Katherine Ashley's
killed fighting for C
Her sole aim is revenge on the man who killed him – the daring Royalist captain Sir Justin Douglas, known as the King's Shadow. Her chance comes unexpectedly early, but when Katherine finds herself facing her sworn enemy, her hatred becomes strangely uncertain. She is suddenly caught up in a sinister web of intrigue. Mysteriously, Justin is always at the centre of the web, so how can Katherine escape? Will she ever discover for herself that revenge is sweet – especially to women?

Also by Judith Polley in Masquerade

The Secret of Val Verde

For My Mother

The King's Shadow

Judith Polley

MILLS & BOON LIMITED
London · Sydney · Toronto

First published 1975 by J. M. Dent & Sons Ltd

This edition published in Great Britain 1977 by Mills & Boon Limited, 17–19 Foley Street, London W1A 1DR

ISBN 0 263 72492 1

Set in 10 on 11pt Plantin

Made and Printed in Great Britain by
C. Nicholls & Company Ltd
The Philips Park Press, Manchester

CHAPTER ONE

THE road from Worcester was crowded with Cromwell's soldiers, often slowing Katherine's coach to a walking pace as it followed in the wake of those fortunate enough to have survived the carnage of the battle which had taken place ten days before. Her blue eyes were clouded with sadness at the pain and misery she witnessed on the homeward journey, adding weight to the silent grief already carried inside her.

Worcester had been a disaster for the Royalist cause. The battle, fought first in the green fields outside the town and then in the streets, was a bloody horror, and there were still visible signs when she arrived two days later after travelling throughout the night to reach the bedside of the man to whom she was betrothed. More than three thousand Royalists killed and six thousand, many of them noblemen, taken prisoner. What a terrible waste of life it had been! So many young men dead – the youth of England! Scores of women, like herself, deprived of happiness through the deaths of their loved ones – and still Charles, defeated, but by birth the rightful King of England, was free to wreak more havoc in the land.

"Why don't I tell the driver to stop at the next inn, mistress? You have not had a good night's sleep in over a week."

A faint smile touched Katherine's drawn face as she looked into the anxious features of her young maid. She was tired. Her eyes burned from lack of sleep and the golden hair escaping from beneath the confines of her bonnet accentuated the pallor of once healthy cheeks. The last inn at which they had halted had been full of soldiers and she had been forced to spend an uncomfortable night in the coach.

"Yes, Sarah, do that. There is nothing for us to hurry back to," she answered, and a heavy sigh escaped her as she turned her attention to the passing countryside. The house at Newbury would be empty. Her father, a major in the army of the Lord Protector, and his men would still be intent on the search for the fugitive Charles. It would be days, perhaps weeks, before he came home. Even then they would keep to their separate rooms, avoiding contact whenever possible and, when together, limiting conversation to the minimum. For over four years since the death of her mother, Katherine and her father had been as strangers. She blamed his harsh ways for the death of her gentle mother and she had vowed never to forgive him.

"The driver says there is an inn a mile ahead," Sarah said, drawing back from the window. "You will feel much better after a night's rest."

Sleep! Katherine thought – if only she could, but as soon as she closed her eyes the dreams would return. Once again she would be sitting at John's side, talking to him throughout the long hours, despite the fact she knew he could not hear her . . . cradling him in her arms in those final moments before he died. Dear, kind John, who was to have become her husband on his next leave from the army – a leave which never took place. Instead of a wedding he had gone to a battle, and in the green fields outside Worcester he and his men had been outnumbered and cut down without mercy by a band of fleeing Royalists.

She had shed many tears when her father related the details, but afterwards anger had engulfed the grief, and with John's death hatred swelled to fill the emptiness inside her. The name of the man who had led the attack was burned into her brain, and with each recollection of it her hatred deepened: Sir Justin Douglas, who was also known as the King's Shadow. Next to Charles he was the most wanted man in England and each day she prayed for his capture. Only when he was dead would John and all the other poor souls who had died that day rest peacefully in their graves.

The King's Shadow! The name was like a peal of golden bells to all supporters of Charles II, for it meant the King was safe. To Cromwell's soldiers it was a death knell. Since Charles had been crowned at Scone, this elusive man had been seen in dozens of places the length and breadth of the country, and the forces of the Lord Protector were taxed to the very limit of their endurance as their generals made futile efforts to have him captured. It was said he was never very far from the side of his royal master, yet neither had so far been caught or been close to capture, and the price on the head of the King's Shadow rose to £700. He was an inspiration to every loyal King's man. Brave and totally dedicated. An excellent swordsman whose exploits were fast becoming a legend.

Katherine thought of the clothes packed in the large coffer at the end of the bed in her room – containing her wedding gown, the trousseau she had spent months embroidering with loving care and the thick gold wedding band she had bought for John only two days before Worcester destroyed the only person she cared for in the whole world.

"Where are we?" She sat up as the carriage came to a standstill, glad of the interruption to her sentimental thoughts. Sentiment was a weakness, her father had often told her before she left Worcester. It was the first time she could ever remember when they had been in agreement.

"We passed through Bristol an hour ago. This place looks clean and quiet. Here, let me help you down." The maid climbed out quickly and reached up for Katherine's hand. "How cold you are! Hurry and come inside."

Katherine shivered as a sharp evening breeze cut through the thin sleeves of her blouse, and she wasted no time in following Sarah into the inn. Apart from a servant sweeping the hearth, the room was deserted. Along one wall were some tables, and Katherine sat down at the one nearest the fire, taking off her gloves and stretching out her cold hands towards the inviting warmth of the flames. To the servant still idly flicking near her with a brush she said:

"Will you bring us something hot to drink, please?"

There was no answer, nor any indication that he had heard them enter. Sarah Parfrey stepped forward and caught his arm, demanding:

"Did you not hear my mistress? She is cold and hungry. Do as you are bid."

A grimy face turned in their direction and dark eyes surveyed the faces of the two women before him; then, without a murmur, he pulled his arm free and went on with what he was doing. Sarah gave an indignant gasp and the colour flooded into her cheeks, staining them a bright pink. She had been Katherine's maid for only six months, but during that short time she had managed to forget she had once been one of four kitchen maids, bullied and harassed by other members of the household who held higher positions. She had hated every hour of the back-breaking toil – every curse rained down on her head – every command which had to be obeyed without question. Most of all she had detested those in authority who had the right to give orders. It never occurred to her that she was rapidly becoming a willing part of everything she professed to hate.

"Don't, Sarah – I do believe the poor man is deaf and dumb," Katherine broke in as her maid looked about to remonstrate with the servant for his atrocious manners. "Go and find someone else to attend us."

"Can I be of service, mistress?" A short, stocky man came through the door leading from the courtyard. "I was feeding the chickens when your carriage drew up. Forgive me for keeping you waiting, but I've so little help these days. My two boys are in the army of the Lord Protector and Jim there" – he motioned to the other man with a grimace – "as you realized, he's deaf and dumb, but he's of my blood and I can hardly turn him out to fend for himself in these hard times. . . . "

"Please." Katherine held up her hand, halting the landlord's flow of speech. "Can you provide us with a hot meal and two rooms for the night?"

"Certainly. Will you take a little mulled wine first to warm you while I prepare the food?"

"That would be most agreeable."

"And while you are eating, I will prepare the rooms. This time last week every one of them was filled with my Lord Cromwell's men, wounded most of them, going home. Have you come far, mistress?"

"From Worcester," Katherine answered quietly.

"Was it as bad as they say? I've heard there was fighting in the streets. And thousands of Royalists killed."

"I wish to God they had all been annihilated. I am very tired, could you please hurry with our food?" Katherine said in a flat tone which deterred further conversation as she turned back towards the fire.

How many years would it be before she could speak – even think – of Worcester without wanting to break down and cry? A year – two – or more, all spent in the empty house at Newbury contemplating what might have been. After the marriage she and John were to have lived with his parents on their farm near Reading. It was not a large place but the land was fertile and gave a good living to those who worked on it, and Katherine knew she would have been happy there. When she was more composed, in a week or so perhaps, she would go and see John's mother and father.

She ate little of the meal placed before her, and the cup of full-bodied wine she drank went straight to her head, making her feel pleasantly drowsy. She was shown to a room at the top of a narrow flight of stairs, where Sarah fussed over her more than usual, but Katherine did not mind on this occasion. Sarah had been a wonderful friend and companion over the past days and had eased her grief many times.

"The bed is hard," the maid grumbled.

Katherine pulled the last of the pins from her hair and allowed it to fall freely about her shoulders. Through the dressing-table mirror, she watched Sarah turn back the covers on the bed.

"And only one blanket – you will freeze to death. Shall I go and find another?"

"No," Katherine said, rising. "It will suffice. Go to bed now – I can manage myself."

For a long while Katherine sat by the bed, vainly searching the Bible open on her lap for some comfort to ease the pain in her heart, but she found none. The one source available could not help her, and she realized she must face the fact that she was alone again.

Leaving the candle still burning, she climbed into bed and

fell asleep immediately, only to awaken some time later, seized with a bout of uncontrollable shivering. Sarah had been right. After ignoring her advice Katherine was loath to wake her and decided to go in search of the landlord herself. Pulling on her robe, she stepped out into the dark passageway which stretched above the full length of the room where she had sat earlier. From the top of the stairs she could see that the fire was almost out, and beside it the deaf and dumb man dozed in a chair. She was about to descend when the door of the inn opened and two men came in, shaking the rain from their coats. Without knowing why, she remained where she was in the shadows, watching them, perhaps too conscious that she was in her night attire to show herself – or was it the furtive way they had entered, so carefully closing the door behind them before crossing to the fireplace, that kept her immobile?

The servant was no longer dozing – or deaf and dumb. Before Katherine's startled gaze he rose to his feet with the litheness of a cat, and without stooping shoulders he was over six feet tall. As he smoothed the black hair back from his dirt-streaked face, she glimpsed hawklike features – saw his relieved expression as he went down on one knee before the newcomers.

"Thank God you are safe. I was afraid my messenger had been caught."

For one breathless moment she felt as if her heart had stopped beating. Who the kneeling figure was she did not know, but she had no difficulty in recognizing the man who commanded his respect. She had been taken by her father to witness the execution of Charles I, to see the fate of those whom God deserted. It was a gruesome affair which she had never been able to forget completely, but now it made possible the identification of the slim young man below her. The resemblance between father and son confirmed that she was staring down at the fugitive King Charles; one of his companions lighted a candle and his face was clearly illuminated. He had the same proud stance, with head thrown slightly back. This boy of twenty-one had been King of England for eight months, a king most of the God-fearing people had rejected. Now he was fleeing for his life. Momentarily Katherine felt a twinge of compassion, but the next moment it was swept away by cold hatred as Charles answered softly:

"As you can see, Justin, I am quite safe. Simon and I rode here without any trouble. Do you realize you dragged me away from the most delightful company of Mistress Jane Lane? I hope it was worth it. Have you found a ship?"

"Not here – we still have far to travel before safe passage to France is ours. Cromwell's men are close on our heels and Colonel Lane's house will be one of the first to be searched. He is known to be a good friend of yours, sire. I had to get you out of there before the place was searched."

"So, once again, the King's Shadow keeps me from the executioner's axe. My thanks, Justin. By God, but you'd have laughed to see me journeying to Bristol. Will Jackson, servant to the Lady Jane, at your service, sir." Charles chuckled, with a mock bow.

Katherine's hands clenched tightly at her sides, her eyes riveted on the figure almost directly below her. The King called him Justin! So this was Sir Justin Douglas, the notorious King's Shadow – the man who had robbed her of a future with John. He did not look like a murderer, but then he was an expert in disguise; his pose as a servant had completely deceived her. He stood straight and tall now, with the air of a man born to command. Her first instinct was to rush downstairs and confront him and give vent to her stifled emotions, but caution and common sense prevailed. Whatever she decided, it was clear she could trust no one but Sarah. For Justin Douglas to be able to pose as a servant could only mean the landlord had Royalist sympathies. Yet another person to shelter him despite the consequences. How popular he was! With the help of her maid she would try to send a message to her father and his men, who were somewhere on the road behind her.

The landlord came into the room carrying a tray laden with bowls of steaming soup and plates of freshly baked bread.

Charles and his companion sat down immediately and began eating. They ate like half-starved animals instead of gentlemen, she thought contemptuously.

"Are you not joining us, Justin?" Charles asked.

"No, sire. I am going to check on two unwelcome guests upstairs," the man replied, and to Katherine's horror he started towards the staircase.

Wheeling about, she stepped quickly back into her room, closing the door as quietly as possible behind her before flinging off her robe and getting into bed. Scarcely had she pulled the clothes high about her face when she heard a faint noise from the doorway and knew that Justin Douglas stood there silently surveying her. She held her breath, beginning to tremble as the minutes passed with interminable slowness, then another quiet click of the door latch told her he had gone. He would also check Sarah's room, she thought. It would be foolish to try and decide on a plan of action until the morning, when she could move about freely again. It was frustrating to know she must wait helplessly until then, but Justin Douglas was a dangerous man and she must be patient or risk losing her chance of having him captured. Sleep claimed her exhausted body and she knew nothing more until morning.

Katherine had washed and dressed herself before Sarah appeared with profuse apologies for oversleeping. Her chatter tailed off into a stunned silence as her mistress sat down and calmly told her of the discovery she had made the previous evening.

"The King – here!"

"England has no king," Katherine reminded her sternly. They were her father's words. Despite the coronation of Charles at Scone in Scotland, he refused to acknowledge anyone other than Oliver Cromwell as the rightful ruler of England.

"I have heard he is a fine man to look on and a good soldier," Sarah said, ignoring the warning look directed at her. "And the men who travel with him are all dedicated to his cause."

"A good soldier! That is why he is at this very moment in

flight from Lord Cromwell's men. As for his looks, yes, he is like his father. No doubt, too, he has the licentious ways of his grandfather, Henri IV of France. As for the men with him, I will have you know one of them is Sir Justin Douglas, the man who murdered John. It will not be easy, but somehow I have to get a message to my father."

"We should wait here for him – "

"And let them escape?" Katherine interrupted. "Last night I heard them talking. When they leave here I am sure they intend to go towards the coast. They mentioned a boat to take them to France. Once they leave, with Justin Douglas leading them, they will be lost to the troops. He is cunning, that one."

"How you must hate him," Sarah said in a troubled voice.

"I have that right." Rising, Katherine picked up her cloak and gloves and turned towards the door. "When you have repacked our things, come and have some breakfast. Perhaps together we can decide what to do."

"It is too dangerous, mistress."

"I have to do something, Sarah. Don't you understand? I have to," Katherine answered with quiet conviction. As she went downstairs she wondered if the young maid was astute enough to have realized her war was not with Charles, but with the man who had stolen her future happiness, and that she was willing to take any risk to bring him to account for his heinous crime.

Katherine's mind worked unceasingly as she ate her breakfast at the same table as she had used the previous evening. Justin Douglas, once again assuming the guise of a deaf and dumb servant, brought her food and shuffled away without even looking into her face. She stifled the disgust which swept over her when he came near and was glad when Sarah joined her. While they ate, two men came out of a back room and sat down near by. Katherine needed only one quick glance to recognize Charles and the fair-haired man who had arrived with him. Nothing about their appearance or actions gave cause for suspicion. Somehow Katherine knew she had to detail them long enough for her father to catch up with them – but how?

Charles rose, and she heard him order the horses to be made ready. As his companion turned towards the door, it opened and a trooper entered. Beyond him she could see another, still mounted and holding the reins of his companion's horse. Katherine caught her breath as the landlord came hurrying forward to attend to him. Sarah's face broke into a smile as they heard him say he had come to commandeer sleeping quarters for the troop of soldiers a day's ride behind him.

"It must be your father," she whispered. "Warn him now. He can fetch help."

"But not in time," Katherine replied in a low, fierce whisper. "And three against two are odds Justin Douglas would enjoy."

"What shall we do then?"

"Go and tell Peter to get the coach ready." Katherine stood up and began to pull on her gloves, aware of the trooper looking curiously around him. A well-disciplined soldier would check travelling passes and that must surely lead to a fight, for Charles and his friends would not have them.

Pausing by the door she looked out at the two dust-streaked horses.

"You have been travelling hard." She forced a smile to her lips as she turned to the man, silently praying her audacious plan would succeed. "Have you by chance news of my father, Major Ashley?"

"How do I know you are his daughter?" The pair of suspicious eyes which raked her from head to toe told her he did not trust her.

"Here is my pass, signed by my father personally." From her purse Katherine took a folded piece of paper and held it out to him. "I was to meet him here, but I fear he has been delayed."

"He's at least two days behind me, Mistress Ashley – that I do know." The trooper's tone was apologetic. "Forgive my brusqueness, but in these times it is hard to trust anyone."

"I quite understand. Some travellers are not always what they seem, are they?"

"It is possible I might see the Major within a day or so. Would you like me to tell him you are waiting here?"

"Thank you for your concern, but I think it will be better if I continue my journey." Katherine motioned to Charles and his companion still standing by the table and her eyes were suddenly full of sadness. "Look at them, my brothers, scarcely twenty and both scarred by the horrors of war. Once they were strong and full of life, now they have the minds of children. There are times when they do not even know me, their own sister. I pray to God my mother's heart will stand the shock of all this." Her voice trembled and she broke off with a heavy sigh. "Forgive me, I did not mean to trouble you with my sorrows – you are a soldier also. You have probably seen far worse casualties. At least they are alive. . . ."

"Have you far to go?"

"To Newbury."

"Then my advice is to stay on the main roads. If you travel across country you will most certainly be stopped." The soldier looked at the two silent figures behind him and then into Katherine's open face, and wished he had a beautiful and devoted sister to minister to his needs. All he had was a miserable wife who made it easy to escape to the war. "Good day, Mistress Ashley. Safe journey to you."

"And to you," Katherine replied, following him to the door.

Out of the corner of her eyes she saw Justin Douglas begin moving towards her. Throughout, the conversation had been loud enough for them all to hear, but she had forgotten him sitting by the fire. She motioned to him to stay back, and remained in the open doorway until the two troopers had ridden off; then she turned and stared at the three men who had stationed themselves so that she could not avoid a confrontation. Justin Douglas was to her left, the fair-haired man on the opposite side, and slightly behind, within easy reach of the door and facing her, Charles stood, hands on his hips. For a moment her courage failed her, then she calmed herself. The first step had been taken and there was no going back.

"Why should the daughter of Major Nathaniel Ashley lie to one of her own kind?" It was Justin Douglas who spoke and she grew pale at the contempt in his voice. It was a shock to know he was acquainted with her father, yet she managed to look at him steadily and answer, despite the gaze of those dark eyes which threatened to invade her most secret thoughts.

"You hear and speak well, sir, for a deaf mute. As for the story I told that poor man, surely my reasons were plain. You – none of you – are what you seem, and I suspect you have no passes."

"And what does that make us in your eyes?" Charles demanded quietly.

As she met his gaze a smile touched the corners of his boyish mouth and she knew he would be the easy one to convince.

"My Lord Cromwell would give much to have his hands on Your Majesty," she murmured and swept down into a curtsy. "I am yours to command."

"The devil you are! The woman's a damned spy," Justin Douglas said in a rough tone.

"Gently, Justin. She has lied for us, remember," the King intervened.

"And for what reason?"

"Why not let her tell us?"

Katherine gazed at the three faces around her. Now she was perfectly calm. For her plan, such as it was, to succeed, she had to win over all three. The difficult one would be Justin Douglas and as yet she did not know how she would deal with him. She suspected he was beyond a woman's wiles, but the other two – both wore sympathetic expressions and she felt a brief moment of triumph. Even kings were susceptible to a woman's smile. She addressed herself to them.

"Why is it men never understand a woman's hatred of war? They find it exciting, even stimulating. They face death without fear and die honourably – and we women have to live with it. We have to nurse them when they are sick or wounded and listen to their continual battle stories – and when they are dead, we have only memories to keep us going." Her blue eyes blazed with bright, angry tears. "What right have you to condemn us to such an existence?"

From the glances they exchanged it was clear that both Charles and his young companion were deeply affected by her words – only Justin Douglas appeared unmoved by the forceful argument. His dark features registered disbelief and Katherine knew he would not be swayed by words alone. Nor would he be influenced by womanly guile. He was the King's Shadow – dangerous and clever. She would do better to ignore him and concentrate on the more susceptible men.

"I suggest we leave this place immediately, sire," Justin said with a fierce frown.

"Without passes you would be stopped by the first patrol who saw you," Katherine returned. "Did you not hear what the trooper said?"

"They will have to catch us first."

"And when you have run your horses into the ground, what will you do then?"

"You have an alternative suggestion?" Charles asked warily.

"Yes. My coach is outside and the pass I carry is made out to allow an unrestricted journey for all those who travel with me. It was originally intended for my coachman and maid only, but as no additional names are specified it could cover whoever is with me. The trooper believed you are my brothers, injured at Worcester. The lie could work again."

"Your father would be proud of you."

Katherine wheeled on Justin Douglas, her face white with anger at his cruel words. Her hatred of him grew with each passing moment.

"I have lost one man at Worcester. If at all possible I want to ensure my father lives out the rest of his life in peace." She wanted to hit out at his hawklike features, despising him for making her lose her temper. Controlling the impulse she turned back to the King. "The death of Your Majesty will no longer serve any useful purpose to the people of this country – we have seen enough bloodshed. Let me help you find a safe house until you can take ship to France."

"I shall come back, Mistress Ashley." Charles's dark eyes challenged her to deny him his right to return. "I am the King."

Katherine lowered her gaze before the burning passion in his eyes. He was the King, and although she did not like it she was one of his subjects and should be more respectful.

"Let me see your pass." Justin Douglas held out his hand and she gave it to him without argument. He read through it and then nodded. "She spoke the truth, but I still don't trust her."

"Are you so loath to give me into the safe keeping of a beautiful woman?" Charles mocked. He looked as if he did not object one iota. "I accept your offer, Mistress Ashley. However, I feel I must warn you my able bodyguard does not trust you. If, as he believes, you have some scheme in mind to deliver me to the Lord Protector, be on your guard. He will not have his head turned by a sweet smile or by those very large inviting blue eyes – innocent though they seem to be."

"My brother allows good judgment to be overruled by a stubborn head." The fair-haired man lifted Katherine's fingers to his lips and his smile was friendly. "I am Simon Douglas, at your service, Mistress Ashley. Rest assured I will do everything in my power to compensate for Justin's boorish manners. He has been too long in the field."

"On behalf of your brother, I accept your apology," Katherine returned. The door opened behind her and Sarah came in. She stopped in amazement at the sight of her mistress's hand still tightly clasped by one of the Royalist fugitives.

"Don't stare, girl! Have you no respect for your King?" Justin Douglas snapped.

Sarah flushed and made a hasty curtsy. Katherine flashed her a warning glance to remain silent, and to her relief the girl contained herself.

"Fetch my trunk down, Sarah. These gentlemen will be travelling with us for a while."

"Allow me," Simon said, and followed the maid upstairs. A few minutes later he reappeared carrying Katherine's baggage. Sarah's face was red with confusion and she did not look at Katherine as she followed her companion out to the coach.

Justin Douglas's face darkened as he watched them together. Sarah was as much under suspicion as herself, Katherine thought – or was there another reason for his anger? When his brother returned to say the coach was ready to leave, he said tersely:

"You would do well to remember we are here to protect the life of the King. Leave that girl alone."

"I have not forgotten my responsibilities, Justin, nor my manners," Simon Douglas returned, and offered his arm to Katherine with a disarming smile. She saw the other man's face darken even more at the gesture, warning her to refuse. Ignoring him, she slipped her hand under Simon's arm and allowed him to escort her outside.

Katherine sat in the coach with Sarah beside her and Charles and Simon Douglas opposite. To her great relief Simon's brother sat up on top with the driver. His presence was unnerving to her. Not only the way he watched her, but the air of arrogance about the man himself was disturbing. She could almost imagine him dressed in fine velvets and lace, being fawned over by the beautiful women who had graced Charles's court. He was a man any woman would be proud to be near – the kind of man who was a stranger to her way of life. She closed her mind against the disturbing pictures invading her thoughts, but it was not possible to shut out the conversation between the younger Douglas and her maid. From the way the boy talked it was clear he idolized his brother. With growing bitterness she was forced to listen to how Justin Douglas had been at the side of his royal master ever since he arrived in England. He had stood at Charles's right hand during the coronation at Scone, travelled south with him, fought by his side during the disastrous battle at Worcester and been instrumental in averting Charles's capture when he was surrounded by Roundhead troops. If it had not been for Justin's brilliant swordsmanship and bravery in fighting his way to the King's side, more than the battle alone would have been lost, Simon related, his voice filled with pride.

Charles appeared to be dozing, oblivious to the conversation, but once or twice when he thought her attentions were elsewhere, Katherine noticed his eyes would open and he would glance quickly out of the window, scanning the road behind them. He would not be taken easily. It had been Katherine's intention to leave Sarah behind at the inn on the pretence of being ill, but Simon Douglas's attentions to the girl made it impossible to speak to her alone without arousing suspicion. Anything she attempted would be perilous. They travelled non-stop throughout the day, and when it grew dark they slept in their seats. At first light Katherine was awake. She sat up and was hastily tidying her appearance when she became aware of Charles watching her.

"Why do you hide such beautiful hair?" he asked as she pushed unruly blonde strands beneath her hat.

"Would Your Majesty have me wear it loose about my shoulders like a scarecrow?" she asked, taken aback.

"Like a scarecrow – no. Like a woman – yes. And those clothes. Have you never hungered after the feel of silk against your skin? Fine lace to adorn your dresses and bright colours? You were not meant to wear sackcloth and ashes."

"I am content with what I have," Katherine returned quietly.

She had to be, with such a strict father. Once she had secretly bought a silk nightgown and had been trying it on when he had discovered her. It had been ripped from her body and the next day he had burnt it in the courtyard before all the servants. She had been confined to her room for a week on a meagre diet and each night he had come to remonstrate with her for the terrible sin she had committed, and to listen to her repentant prayers. She had never forgotten – nor forgiven – nor had she quite understood why it was a sin to want to be beautiful.

The coach slowed to a halt. She looked out of the window, expectantly searching for her coachman, and found only one man on top. The familiar profile which turned in her direction sent a chill of fear down her spine.

"Peter!" At the alarm in her voice Charles opened the door and leapt down. Hesitantly she followed and found herself staring up into the mocking features of Justin Douglas. He wore the coachman's coat and hat, but of Peter there was no sign.

"What have you done with him?" she demanded.

"He left us late last night," came the infuriatingly calm reply. "Don't worry, he will suffer no worse than a few bruises and a headache."

"How dare you handle one of my servants so – so despicably?" Katherine found herself fumbling for words. He had quietly and effectively disposed of her only source of help. She had sadly underestimated his intelligence – and her own capabilities. What yesterday had appeared a positive course of action, now presented itself as a disastrous mistake.

Justin Douglas climbed down and faced her. The scrutiny of those dark eyes made her feel very uncomfortable.

"When your servant is found and questioned, he will direct the soldiers towards the coast, the direction we are facing now. Which is what I want. We shall be long gone in the other direction. If you will get back in, sire, we will continue. Mistress Ashley . . . " He took Katherine by the arm and helped her back inside. Their eyes met and locked. She fell back in her seat inwardly shaking, sickened by the knowledge that she was trapped in a web of her own lies. The man she had set out to snare had ensnared her, leaving her no option but to continue with her deception. . . .

CHAPTER TWO

THROUGHOUT the day the coach driven by Justin Douglas continued along the Salisbury road. Katherine racked her brains to find some solution to the problem suddenly facing her, but none was apparent. She prayed they would be stopped by soldiers, but even that did not happen, and as dusk fell her spirits lagged. It had all been for nothing. She had set out to trap the man responsible for the death of her betrothed, but here she was, little more than a prisoner in her own coach, with no idea of her destination.

They were changing direction now, leaving the road and going across country. Her eyes centred on the gigantic stone columns up ahead. Stonehenge! They were crossing Salisbury Plain. What game was Justin Douglas playing now? Did he not realize they were scarcely more than four miles from the garrison at Salisbury?

"Don't look so alarmed, Mistress Ashley – Justin knows what he is doing," Charles murmured. "He and I have shared many uncomfortable moments over the past weeks, but I know his loyalty and his friendship are beyond question. In many ways I am a lucky man."

"I am meant to be on my way to Newbury," she protested. "If we are stopped – "

"You will say you are making a detour to Winchester to visit a sick friend."

"Winchester! You will find no shelter there." Yet why should such a careful man as Justin Douglas risk the life of his royal master unless he had allies there to help him?

"Justin has his reasons. I am in good hands and I have learned not to question what he does."

"A king should not place his life in the hands of one man,"

Katherine said, wishing she did not care what happened to this likeable young man. Had he remained a name without a face she would not have cared, but since their meeting she had been remembering the death of his father, and the memory was not pleasant. He did not deserve to die because his birthright had made him the ruler of England. To her shame she realized she was beginning to hope his son might succeed in his daring attempt to escape to France.

Charles smiled across at her, his dark eyes serious with secret thoughts.

"Justin is worth a dozen men. If Cromwell had the like of him I would indeed fear for my life."

"Are you not afraid of being caught? Of death?" The King's admiration of his bodyguard made Katherine feel uneasy. Such trust! Such friendship! She had never shared anything so intense with anyone.

Charles looked at her from beneath drawn brows and she saw not the face of a boy of twenty-one, but that of a man who lived daily with the knowledge he would follow his father to the execution block if captured.

"At Scone, just eight short months ago, I was crowned. I came south with more than nine thousand hardy Scotsmen. Barely a quarter of that number ever returned to their families and homes. Do you know how I have spent the days since Worcester, Mistress Ashley? Hiding in ditches, stealing food, living like an animal instead of a man – let alone a king. If it had not been for – unexpected help, I would have been captured long ago. I have no stomach for this kind of life; I was born to rule, to fight those who dispute my right – not to live like a pack rat. Three nights ago I slept, or tried to sleep, in an oak tree, while Cromwell's troopers beat the bushes below me. A poor bed for a king, do you not agree? I have seen death and feared it, but I must live with it, and to do that I have to accept it as part of my existence. If I died tomorrow, you might say there would be few to mourn my passing, and perhaps you would be right. But for those few, men who have already died for me, men like Justin and his brother who protect me with their lives and ask nothing in return, I must not think of death or even defeat. My father was many things to many men – some good, some bad, but to me he was the greatest man I have ever known or am likely to know, whatever the span of my lifetime. One day I will sit in my rightful place on the throne of England and those who murdered him will grovel at my feet begging for mercy."

"Is it your rightful heritage you seek, or revenge?" Katherine asked, and immediately knew she had gone too far.

Charles's handsome face grew cold and he turned away from her indicating the conversation was at an end. Without knowing why, Katherine felt near to tears. His confession had touched her. If he had been playing on her sympathy, he had succeeded.

On the far side of Salisbury Plain the coach was brought to a halt outside an inn. The only thing she could think of as Justin Douglas helped her out was how quickly she could have something hot to eat.

"I've driven the horses as hard as I can – we must risk staying here overnight," Justin said as they paused before the door. The cloak he had borrowed from Charles made him look more respectable. He draped the dusty coachman's jacket around the King's shoulders with a tight smile. "It's your turn to play the servant now, sire. If any questions are asked, Mistress Ashley, you are visiting friends in Winchester. No – perhaps it would be better to say the family of the man you lost at Worcester. It would take a callous man to question you further after that."

"I know of one," Katherine said, between tight lips.

His smile mocked her, but there was no amusement in his eyes, and she suddenly realized he was deliberately provoking her in the hope that she would confirm his suspicions.

"A woman who mourns her man for more than a week is rare in my estimation," he said, and opened the door for her to enter.

He took charge of ordering a meal and accommodation for the night. As they were the only travellers, there was no difficulty with rooms. Simon Douglas and Sarah sat at a different table, and Katherine realized she would have to reprimand her maid for the uncomely interest she was showing in the fugitive Royalist. She was obviously attracted to him, but they came from vastly different backgrounds, and nothing worth while would be gained by allowing the association to continue.

Katherine ate her food in silence while Justin Douglas and Charles engaged in unimportant chatter. She made no attempt to join in, and when she had finished her meal she did not linger. Since her somewhat heated words with the King, she had been pointedly ignored. It was humiliating.

"Will you be ready for an early start in the morning?" Justin Douglas followed her upstairs and opened the door to her room.

"An early start for where? You are risking more than your own lives if you continue to use my coach for your wild schemes. You have taken advantage of my offer of help, sir, and I will go no farther with you." Katherine tossed her hat onto the bed and pulled the pins from her hair. She had not had it cut since she was a child, and it streamed past her shoulders almost to her waist, like a cloud of golden sunlight against the dark material of her dress.

"Must we be constantly at each other's throats?" She turned in surprise to find that he had closed the door and now stood with his back against it. She stifled a sudden rush of apprehension as his dark eyes contemplated her boldly. What now? More taunts – or accusations?

"You have left me little alternative with your rudeness," she returned stiffly, and he smiled. How different he looked when those hard features softened!

"My brusque manner – like your coldness – is a mere front, but one I consider necessary in order to protect the King. I shall trust no man or woman, not even old friends, until my charge is safely *en route* for France."

Katherine was about to ask what he meant by her coldness "being a mere front" and then changed her mind. This was the first time he had shown any friendliness towards her. It could be another act meant to lure her into a false sense of security, or perhaps it was a genuine change of attitude and he regretted his earlier manner. Either way she was prepared.

"I accept your apology. Now will you please allow me to go to bed?" She hoped he did not notice the tremor in her voice.

"Tomorrow you must travel with us." He moved towards her and, without knowing why, she stepped back. His smile grew. "I see you do not trust easily either, but rest assured my reason for following you is not what you imagine."

Katherine almost choked at his insolence, but she could not deny his presence was making her decidedly uncomfortable. The way he looked at her was unnerving. John had never stared at her so, and she was to have been his wife. The memory of the dead man helped to clear her brain. Turning away, she opened her overnight bag and began to take out a few toilet requisites, trying to calm the wild beating of her heart.

"Perhaps you will send my maid to me when you go downstairs?" It was a polite dismissal, but Justin Douglas did not move.

"You are angry and you have every right to be," he said quietly. "Will you forget me and think of the King? You wanted to help – "

"That was before you brought me here – miles from my true destination. I have risked too much already . . . I cannot help you further." Katherine tried to sound indignant.

"I did not believe you when you said you were sick of the killing. I didn't even accept the fact someone you loved had been killed at Worcester, but I do now. I have to believe you because I need your help to get the King safely to Winchester. Once there you can go your own way." He was so close to her that as she turned, his face was barely inches from hers and she saw nothing there to tell her it was a trick. She felt exhilarated by the victory.

"Why?" She had to ask the question – so much depended on his answer. Already her mind was racing.

"I am convinced the daughter of Major Nathaniel Ashley would not betray her father's cause without good reason. I was a fool to try and see a more devious motive for what you have done, and I would not blame you if you refused my request."

Yes, she had good reason, Katherine thought, and when he was in chains in prison she would tell him what it was. His capture was more important than that of the King. She wanted him dead for what he had done.

"How can I help you?"

"Allow us to ride in the coach as far as Winchester and use those pretty blue eyes to persuade any inquisitive soldiers who may stop us that we are all we say we are."

Katherine lowered her eyes and fixed them on the broad chest of the man directly before her. He had discarded the cloak, and the grey shirt he wore was open at the front, revealing a heavy gold locket on a long chain around his neck. It probably held a picture of a woman, she thought, his wife – or a mistress. She wanted to open it and gaze at the face of a woman who could love the kind of man who killed without quarter.

"You have a persuasive tongue, but I'll go no farther than Winchester. I dare not," she said and prayed he could not hear her loud heart beats.

Justin Douglas took her hand and raised her fingers to his lips. Somehow she suppressed the impulse to snatch them from his grasp. He continued to hold them and look at her, a smile tugging at the corners of his lean mouth. She could not deny he was an attractive man and far more dangerous than she had ever foreseen.

"One day you will be repaid for all you have done," he murmured.

"As I'm sure you will," Katherine returned. His friendliness made her bolder and she ventured to ask: "Have you friends in Winchester who will hide you?"

The dark eyes gleamed. "I tell no one of my plans, not even the King. It is better not to involve yourself too deeply."

"Take care, there are spies everywhere." Katherine broke off, hoping she sounded convincing. "My father has paid informers all over the country. He is as dedicated to the Lord

Protector as you are to the King and, since John's death, to capture King Charles has become his sole aim in life."

"John? Was he the man who died?"

"Yes." Quickly Katherine withdrew from his grasp. He turned towards the door, paused and looked back as if troubled by her words.

"You need have no fear your help will be misused. My home is five miles from Winchester – the King will be safe there for a few days."

How long Katherine stared after him she did not know. She could not believe her good fortune. When Sarah came in later to prepare her mistress for bed, she found her busily writing. Katherine wrote steadily for a few more minutes, then folded the paper and stood up. Her cheeks were flushed. At first Sarah thought she was feverish and then realized that Katherine's eyes were wet with tears.

"What is it?" she cried. "I saw one of them follow you – "

"The King is going to stay at the home of Justin Douglas near Winchester. I have written it all down here." Katherine held out the note. "Give it to the landlord with this gold piece. He must have someone take it to Colonel Sandford in Winchester."

Sarah took the letter and stared at it wide-eyed. It was obvious that she was imagining her young beau under arrest.

"Simon Douglas is a fugitive – he must take his chances like all the others." Katherine's tone reproved Sarah's indecision. "Do as you are told at once. Pretend I want some hot milk if you are questioned. Now go."

Turning away she began to undress, not giving her maid an opportunity to argue. Colonel Sandford was in command of the troopers in the immediate area; he was also a close friend of her father's and often came to dine with them at their home. Her signature on the letter would be sufficient to tell him the information was genuine. If all went well, tomorrow would see the end of her quest. She could go on to Newbury knowing Justin Douglas and his friends had been captured.

Pulling a wrap over her nightgown she sat down on the edge of the bed. The violence of her hatred for the man both shocked and alarmed her. Never before had she allowed emotion to rule her actions – or drive her to such extremes. He was a clever man and sincere in his devotion to the King, but the measures he took to protect him were unforgivable. Her father had often spoken of men who enjoyed wars and the excitement of the fighting and killing. She believed Justin Douglas to be such a person.

Sarah returned and without a word went across to the dressing-table, picked up the silver-backed brush there and began to brush her mistress's long hair. Her silence indicated she did not approve of Katherine's scheme.

"The landlord has the note?"

"Yes, Mistress Katherine. The stable boy will deliver it to Colonel Sandford within the hour."

"Good, I think I shall sleep soundly tonight. You don't approve of what I have done, do you? Shame on you, Sarah, to be taken in by good looks and a smooth tongue."

"I – I didn't expect them to be so – so kind," the maid stammered. "And Sir Justin – he is so totally dedicated to the King, not at all the kind of man I had expected. Your father often speaks of the licentious lives these Royalists lead – but he, he seems different."

"It is only a pose. Have you forgotten he is an expert in deception?" Katherine said drily. "And remember his brother shares the same blood."

"He is not like his brother. Sir Justin is a professional soldier as his father was before him."

"Was Simon Douglas at Worcester?"

"Yes."

"Then how can you say they are not alike?" Katherine wheeled on her angrily. "Most likely he was at his brother's side when John's troop was attacked and wiped out. Fifteen men against eight, and no quarter given. I forbid you to talk of him to me again. I will be glad when we are home and you can put him out of your mind. Open the window and then go to bed."

Sarah's face took on a stubborn expression, and for a moment Katherine expected her to argue, then she turned to do as she was told. She looked down into the courtyard as she reached for the window catch and gave a startled gasp.

"Mistress – soldiers!"

Katherine was at her side in an instant. There were a dozen of them, watering their horses. They did not show any inclination to come inside, and she realized that once their mounts had been refreshed they would carry on – probably to Winchester. Suddenly she caught her breath.

"Sarah – look, isn't that Captain Grahaeme? It can't be, I left him in Worcester with father."

Sarah leant up on tiptoe, nodding after awhile.

"Yes, mistress, it is. What luck! He will help us. He has always been very fond of you."

For a price, Katherine thought in silent anguish. A stolen kiss – a furtive caress, hoping no one would come upon them. Her eyes clouded as she stared down at the tall, red-headed soldier in charge of the troopers. Francis Grahaeme, John's elder brother. Never had two brothers had so little in common. Francis had despised John's gentleness and quiet nature and laughed at the placid, passionless courtship he had shared with Katherine. She knew he was the kind of man her father would have preferred her to marry, for the army was his life too. Francis Grahaeme was cold, calculating, very ambitious and totally without scruples, although she suspected a blind eye was turned against his womanizing ways because of the many commendations he had received throughout his years of service. Oliver Cromwell himself had spoken of his great courage during the campaign in Ireland and had personally hastened his promotion. Poor John had lived in his elder brother's shadow. She had never told him of Francis's attentions whenever they were alone, although at times they had become almost unbearable, for she was afraid an argument might result between the two brothers. John was a farmer by choice, a soldier by necessity and no match for the brother whose aggressive nature found an outlet in fighting and war. Francis and Justin Douglas were a matched pair, she thought bitterly. She hesitated for a moment only. Much as she disliked Francis, she hated the other man more. Nothing and no one must turn her from her objective now. Her eyes narrowed sharply as she stared down into the courtyard, and a distinct pallor crept into her cheeks.

"That isn't the landlord talking to them." Her voice trailed off into a horrified silence. "It's your friend, Simon Douglas. Why is he taking such a risk? My letter! Sarah, you swear you gave it to the landlord?"

"Yes. He promised to send it at once."

"Something is wrong. I cannot wait any longer. Run downstairs and tell Captain Grahaeme I am here. Let us see what the King's Shadow can do faced with twelve good fighting men."

"Obviously the sight of my being cut down would give you great satisfaction, but for the moment the pleasure must be postponed."

The bedroom door was wide open behind them and Justin Douglas stood there, Charles at his side. As Katherine stood stunned, the former reached into his shirt and pulled out the letter she had written. The murderous look in his eyes made her inwardly shudder.

"Always give a spy enough rope . . . " he said meaningly. His voice was like tempered steel. "How many times before have you led unsuspecting men into the arms of enemy troops, Mistress Ashley?"

She blanched and swayed back from him. Her best chance now lay with the soldiers in the courtyard and she spun around, her lips parting in a scream as she threw herself at the window.

"The maid, sire," she heard Justin Douglas say. The next moment she was seized bodily and wrenched backwards. Her cry for help died beneath the hand clapped roughly over her mouth. She raked upwards with her nails at the face above her and heard a savage oath; then her hands were caught together in a fierce grip, and the weight of Justin Douglas's body crushed her against the wall and she was helpless.

"Keep still or I'll knock you cold," came the grim warning and she knew it was useless to continue the fight. He had deliberately given her news of his intended plans, knowing what she would do. He had not trusted her from the beginning, but she, fool that she was, in her eagerness to see him caught, had allowed herself to be persuaded by his glib sincerity – and only a short while before she had chided Sarah for the same foolishness.

Hot tears stung her eyes. Angry, bitter tears. Still holding her fast, her captor eased away slightly and peered cautiously out of the window.

"Damnation! One of them is coming inside." He turned and looked down at Katherine, one cheek lined with two bloody scratches from her nails. "Before he finds us, you and I will have a reckoning, mistress."

"No, Justin, she is not to be harmed."

Charles released Sarah and thrust her down on the bed, motioning her to be quiet, but she started up, determined to protect her mistress.

"The captain downstairs is a friend of Mistress Katherine's. If you dare lay a finger on her, he will hunt you down like a dog," she cried venomously.

"Will he now?" Justin Douglas's tone was dangerously low. He did not release Katherine, in fact his grip on her tightened. She almost fainted at the murderous expression on his face. "Who is he?"

"Captain Grahaeme. He is a close friend."

Katherine lowered her gaze beneath her captor's burning eyes. The implication in them was only too plain, and she felt her cheeks slowly begin to flood with colour.

"Sire, do you have your pistol?" Justin nodded in satisfaction as Charles produced a weapon. "Please be good enough to stand by the window and let me know if Mistress Ashley's friend is still outside."

"No – I can see no captain. He must have been the one who came inside."

"He has no reason to search up here, but I fear Simon's impersonation of the landlord will not withstand prolonged scrutiny. Go downstairs and get rid of him, Mistress Ashley. I don't care how you do it – use all your charm to send him on his way."

Katherine gasped and gathered her robe closer about her as she was released.

"How dare you suggest I – I be nice to him in order to help you? You are quite mad."

"Mad or not, you had better believe me when I say I am quite prepared to sacrifice not only my own life and yours to get the King to safety, but also hers." He turned and looked directly at Sarah, who cowered back on the bed, wide-eyed and terrified.

"You would not – could not be so heartless," Katherine whispered disbelievingly, but deep in her heart she knew he would do whatever was necessary. If she refused his demands Sarah would surely suffer injury or death in the clash which would follow when the troopers stormed upstairs.

"Very well, I will try, but I can guarantee nothing."

"I was under the impression you knew him quite well," Justin said significantly as he followed her to the door. Her colour deepened. One day he would pay a hundredfold for all these insults.

"He – he is John's brother – " She broke off, angry, humiliated, frightened at the confrontation to come.

As she stood on the landing, every fibre of her body cried out for her to rush downstairs and reveal the hiding-place of the most wanted fugitives in the country, to think of nothing but the capture of the King's Shadow, but she could not – not while Sarah remained with them as their prisoner.

Francis Grahaeme was enjoying a tankard of ale as she hesitantly descended the stairs, hugging her wrap tightly around her neck. His eyes had the habit of undressing her, silently mocking the shyness which had first attracted John to her side.

"Captain Grahaeme – Francis." She forced a smile to her stiff lips as he spun around with an oath. "I was right, it is you. I saw you arrive from my bedroom window. Is it too much to hope my father will be arriving soon?" It was the only excuse she could think of which sounded plausible. She had completely forgotten that she was miles from her original destination.

"Katherine! In God's name . . . what are you doing here?" Pale green eyes, whose insipid colour she had always hated, dwelt on her in amazement. He was a good head taller than she was, with broad shoulders that went well with the uniform. He often boasted it was his build which first attracted women, with the uniform taking second place. "Why are you not at home?"

Home! Katherine thought distractedly. Newbury!

"We have been plagued by troubles, Francis, ever since the coach left Worcester." Somehow she managed to calm the wild beating of her heart and kept smiling as she moved past him towards the fire where Simon Douglas stood watching her in open-mouthed surprise. She darted a warning look at him, and he turned on his heel and slouched away, muttering something about bringing up a fresh cask of wine from the cellars.

"Your pass was made out for Newbury, not Winchester."

Katherine spun around and stared with raised eyebrows into the handsome features before her.

"I am the daughter of Nathaniel Ashley, not some serving wench or a fugitive from justice. I do not have to answer to anyone for my comings and goings."

"Only to your father, and – in his absence – to me. I am his second-in-command now, my fine Katherine, and if I ask you why you are here, you will tell me. Won't you?" It was more of a veiled threat than a question, and she knew it was useless to try and evade the question further.

"Very well, if you insist. Peter, my coachman, was taken ill on the road. I stopped and hired another coachman – a fool as it turned out, who lost his way and ended up here. No sooner had I gone upstairs to bed than he ran off, leaving us stranded. The landlord is arranging for another driver to take his place in the morning. I only pray he will be more competent."

"Poor Katherine, so much unnecessary trouble in your hour of grief," Francis Grahaeme chuckled. "When I didn't overtake your coach on the road I was beginning to think you had really taken my brother's death to heart and done away with yourself. I am relieved to hear otherwise."

"I loved John," Katherine said scathingly, restraining the urge to hit out at his grinning face. "I would have preferred you to have been in his place . . . he was too . . . too . . . "

"Good to die? Yes, he was rather righteous, wasn't he? And look where it got him." The sensuous mouth deepened into a sardonic smile, mocking her indignation. "We must see more of each other when I get back to Newbury. Your father has generously offered me lodgings in his house. We shall go riding together whenever I have the free time – I remember you ride well, Katherine. It is one of the many qualities in you that I find attractive – your ability to do everything so well. In time I think we shall become . . . friends . . . "

Time! She had plenty of that, Katherine thought miserably, and for an instant the awful knowledge she was to share the house with John's loathsome brother made her forget the fugitives hiding in her bedroom. She felt like a trapped animal, transferred from one cage to another. John could have freed her, but he was dead, and if she was not mistaken Francis intended to take his place. It was not a pleasant assumption.

"You did not tell me about my father." She stepped to one side, but he also moved, barring her way back to the staircase. "Is he coming here too?"

"No, he is a day or so behind me at least and on his way to Winchester. We have received reports that the fugitive Charles has been seen there. I am to hold my men outside the town in case this is true and he tries to escape. This time I think we might catch him."

"I – I wish you luck," Katherine murmured, and again tried to go past him. She was seized in a firm embrace and drawn against Francis's chest despite her protests.

"Let me go! I have told you before I am not one of your tavern wenches!" she cried angrily, fighting to free her hands.

"You will be whatever I want you to be – now," came the chilling answer.

Now! Now John was no longer about to protect her – now Francis was her father's right hand. In disgust she tried to turn her face away, but it was too late, and for a long torturing moment she was forced to endure the pressure of his mouth on hers.

"There now, wasn't it better being kissed by a real man instead of a weakling boy?" Francis released her with a low laugh and, picking up his helmet, strode towards the door. "I shall look forward to our next meeting in Winchester. Good-bye, Katherine."

She did not answer, but fled upstairs as soon as the door slammed shut behind his departing figure, only to find Justin Douglas standing out of sight in a shadowy alcove at the top of the landing. The contempt blazing out of his eyes told her he had witnessed everything. Without a word she returned to her room. Let him think what he liked – why should she care?

"They are leaving." Charles still stood by the window. "What now, Justin?"

"You have always been led by me, sire – pray continue to be so now. I know exactly what has to be done, but I need Mistress Ashley here to help me carry it off. Do not fear I will harm her – I would not soil my hands by taking her worthless life."

"You were not so particular at Worcester when you cut down the man I was to have married." Katherine spat the words at him, and the hatred blazing out of her lovely, tear-streaked face at last revealed to him the true reason for her trickery.

"Justin is no more responsible for his death than I am, or any of my men who were there," Charles informed her coldly.

"John lived long enough to tell my father what happened. He and his men, eight in all, were chasing some fleeing Royalists when they were set upon and surrounded by twice their number – led by you." She glared at Justin Douglas, and cursed the quirk of fate that had decreed she should be a woman and not a man able to take up arms and mete out justice to those who had brought her such heartache. "No quarter – that was the order you gave. You slaughtered them all like the butcher you are."

"I think you have said enough." The red scratches she had made stood out on the sudden pallor of Justin Douglas's skin. "Men are killed in war. No one wants it to happen. I remember the incident; I have cause to, although it did not happen as you relate it."

"I prefer to believe the words of a dying man," Katherine retorted, and he shrugged indifferently.

"No matter. Sire, will you find Simon and tell him to make the coach ready again, and then will you bring up Mistress Ashley's trunk? Our plans need a little rearranging."

Charles nodded. He hesitated for a moment, his eyes on Katherine who stood with head downbent, rubbing her bruised wrists; he was obviously disturbed by her distress. Sensing the King's mood, his companion said quickly:

"Time is suddenly very important, sire. Please do as I ask."

Katherine watched in silence as her overnight bag was tipped out onto the bed and, after that, the contents of her purse. Certain items were put aside from the rest. The King returned with Simon, carrying her trunk between them. That too was opened and from it Justin Douglas took a dark-coloured dress and bonnet and a cloak. He stared at them thoughtfully, then at Charles and finally at Katherine.

"It should work – even though you are taller. You, sire, are about to become Mistress Ashley. Dressed in her clothes and with her maid, Simon will drive you, in her coach, to our home. What could be more simple? Her pass is signed by the Major himself, which will certainly carry some weight if you are stopped, and if you pretend you have a fever and let the girl do all the talking, I doubt if you will have any trouble. They are looking for three men, not two women and a coachman."

"And you, Justin?" Charles asked. He held the dress against him and grimaced. "What will you do?"

"It is a known fact we are always together, so if I am seen it will be assumed you are my companion. In your clothes Mistress Ashley will make a fine boy."

Katherine leapt to her feet, her face scarlet at the audacious suggestion. Was there no end to the humiliation he inflicted on her?

"You cannot force me to go with you."

"I can make you do anything I wish," Justin Douglas

er. "When you have changed, sire, Simon will bring clothes. By morning I want to be well away from

"I won't leave my mistress," Sarah said bravely.

"Simon will take care of you, and this time he won't play the gentleman if you attempt any more tricks," she was told, and she glanced at Katherine miserably.

When Simon returned with Charles's discarded clothes, Justin took them and tossed them onto Katherine's lap.

"Put them on."

"And if I refuse?" she challenged. Charles did not want her harmed. If she was stubborn, they would have no alternative but to leave her behind. Justin Douglas stepped over to the bed, and the expression on his face left her in no doubt as to the seriousness of his intentions when he said tersely:

"If you refuse, I shall tear off those clothes and dress you myself. You have five minutes." Turning on his heel he left her struggling for an answer.

CHAPTER THREE

KATHERINE looked down at the rough homespun shirt and breeches lying across her knees and wished she had sufficient courage to refuse to dress as a boy in order to take the place of the fugitive King Charles, but the strain of the past week was beginning to take its toll of both her strength and spirit. John's death had been a crushing blow to the plans she had made for a future away from a tyrannical father and the house he ruled with an iron fist. Her one consolation had been in the hope of somehow bringing John's murderer to justice, but she had failed miserably in that and was now a prisoner of the very man she had sought to have captured.

"Mistress Katherine, please change your clothes, or that awful man will do as he threatened. I saw it in his eyes," Sarah pleaded.

Katherine nodded. At least she would not give Justin Douglas the pleasure of humiliating her further. When her tormentor returned, she was dressed. He tossed down a pair of well-worn boots.

"Not bad. Put these on too. They are a little large but you will be riding most of the time."

"And any discomfort I suffer will not prick your conscience one tiny bit," she said scathingly.

"Think of the great service you are rendering to your King," he returned, his voice heavy with sarcasm.

"If I were a man you would not dare force me to endure this degradation," Katherine said, pulling on the boots.

"If you were a man you would be dead after such treachery," Justin Douglas said in a rough tone.

She stood up, facing him, and her blue eyes blazed defiance.

She was beaten for the moment and her spirit was weak but by no means broken, as he would find out to his cost.

"I am surprised you hesitate when it comes to killing a woman."

"I have never found myself in a situation which demanded such drastic measures – until now. I will go to hell and back and take you with me if it means the King safely reaches France. You have forfeited all the usual courtesies afforded women and you must accept the consequences. Expect no mercy from me, for you will get none. If you speak out of turn I will gag you, and any attempt to escape will find you tied in the saddle."

"My father will kill you for this." Katherine was appalled by his callousness.

"And save the public executioner a task? I doubt it, not even for his own daughter. Surely you don't want to miss the bloody spectacle of my head rolling in the dirt, after all your efforts to have me captured? What a man this John must have been to arouse such passion." He stepped close to her, staring with narrowed eyes into her ashen face. "If you truly loved him as deeply as you want me to believe, then I'm sorry for you, but I don't believe you did. The scene I witnessed downstairs was not that of a grief-stricken woman being comforted by her lover's brother. Far from it. In my estimation you are incapable of any deep feelings. I think you seek revenge not for his death, but in order to appease your wounded pride. I've known women like you before. They can't bear to let go of anything – money, jewels or men – once they have them in their possession. The desire to be revenged at any cost becomes a fever in their blood."

Katherine's open palm caught him a stinging blow across one cheek. She expected anger in return and was dismayed when all he did was laugh.

"You would go down well at Drury Lane, mistress."

"Justin – how do I look?"

Charles stood in the doorway, grinning broadly, giving no sign he might have witnessed what had happened. Simon Douglas entered behind him and took Sarah by the arm. Katherine was instantly alarmed at the thought that her maid might suffer for her mistakes, and her own plight was momentarily forgotten.

"Such a comely wench will have no trouble with the soldiers," Justin drawled after a close inspection. The King was certainly taller than Katherine, but with the hood of the cloak pulled well around his face and seated in the coach, he would pass without difficulty as a woman. One more victory to the King's Shadow, Katherine thought bitterly.

"Let me stay with my mistress!" Sarah pleaded.

"No, you are a necessary part of the charade. Behave yourself and no harm will befall you," Justin told her coldly.

"You cannot blame her for my actions," Katherine broke in. "She was obeying my orders. Let her go, please. She will not betray you. I swear it."

"So you are capable of some small feeling," Justin said, glancing at her quickly. "However, it changes nothing. The girl is in your charge, Simon. When you are dreaming of sweet words to whisper in her ear, remember it was she who was entrusted with the letter meant to bring the troops here."

"If she had refused I would have dismissed her immediately," Katherine said, and knew none of them believed her.

She was locked in the room while Justin Douglas escorted the others to the coach waiting in the courtyard. She watched it drive off, and then as he turned away and began saddling the horses she looked desperately around the room. He had thought of everything. Her trunk and overnight bag had both been repacked and taken away – Charles was even carrying her purse. She was left with nothing but the clothes she was wearing.

It seemed an eternity before he came back. She stood defiantly in the middle of the room, but suddenly she was feeling far from brave.

"Are you ready?"

"Where are you taking me?"

"We will find somewhere to camp for the rest of the night – after that – " He shrugged. "Plait that hair and put on your cloak. Keep your head covered at all times."

"It would spoil your plans if I was seen to be a woman, wouldn't it?" Katherine knew as she plaited her hair that he had shown her the opportunity she had been seeking, but the brief gleam of hope was rudely extinguished as he said:

"Either you keep your head covered or I crop your hair. The choice is yours."

In silence Katherine did as she was told. After a long scrutinizing look around the room, he took her by the arm and led her downstairs.

"One moment before we go."

He stopped and unlocked the cellar door. A light burned at the bottom of the stairs and Katherine could just make out the bound figures of the stable lad and the landlord. To them she was a shadowy figure beside Justin Douglas, and the implication of his action became clear. His grasp on her arm tightened as she tried to move forward, and his expression warned her to silence.

"Come, sire, we have a long way to go," he said and swung the door closed again before she could speak.

"You can't leave them like that."

"The boy's bonds were deliberately left loose." He led her out to the horses and helped her to mount, holding fast to the reins of her horse while he did so. "By the morning the troopers in Winchester will know the King was here – as you intended."

"And after what you said they will follow us," Katherine whispered, "not the coach."

He nodded, with a tight smile. It was almost midnight as they rode away from the inn and turned their horses along the road the coach had travelled earlier. Katherine drew her cloak closer around her cold body, knowing it was fear and not the wind which chilled her. He was deliberately retracing their steps, knowing that somewhere along the way they must encounter Roundhead troops. He was making a determined effort to decoy them away from Winchester – away from the King whose life was more important to him than his own or hers, and there was no way she could stop him. He was the bravest and the most frightening man she had ever encountered.

The ground where Katherine lay was wet with early morning dew. In the sunlight it glistened on the branches of the trees overhead and on the leaves of the thick foliage of bushes and ferns a few feet away. Her cloak was soaked with it. A tall figure loomed over her as she stretched her cramped limbs; still only half awake, she was stirred none too gently with the toe of a boot.

"It's time to go," Justin Douglas said and moved past her to finish saddling the horses. She had lain awake for hours, hoping he would sleep first and give her a chance to escape, but he had seated himself beneath a tree, deliberately positioning himself between her and the mounts. He was almost hidden from her view and she had not known whether he was awake or sleeping. She had eventually fallen into an exhausted sleep just before dawn.

She climbed to her feet, shivering in the keen air, to find he was holding out his cloak to her.

"Put this on until yours is dry."

She took it without a word of thanks and pulled it around her. From his saddlebag he took a leather doublet and slipped it over his shirt. He appeared neither cold nor tired. He would have to sleep some time, Katherine realized, but then so would she. Of the two of them she knew he was the one who would survive the longest. She was a good horsewoman, but that was all. Already her limbs felt weak with the cold and she was not looking forward to the prospect of sleeping out in the open again.

"Where are we?"

"On the outskirts of Salisbury Plain. Mount up, Mistress Ashley."

This time he made no attempt to help her, and she pulled herself into the saddle very slowly, wanting to give the impression of being tired and miserable. As he turned away from her and bent to adjust one of his stirrups, she dug her heels into her horse's flanks and galloped off, passing so close to him that he was forced to throw himself to one side to avoid being ridden down.

The trees ahead looked less dense, and she headed in that direction. If only she could find the road, he would not dare follow her out into the open. The wind caught her cloak and dragged it from her shoulders, snatching at the hood and wrenching it from her head so that her hair tumbled free about her shoulders. The forest gave way to open land, but there was no sign of the road. She reined in, not knowing which way to turn, and then she heard the drumming of hooves and Justin Douglas's large black horse came crashing out of the undergrowth behind her.

At a reckless pace she urged her horse across open country, helpless tears blinding her vision as he drew steadily closer. No matter how she wheeled and turned he closed the gap between them, and too late she realized he was forcing her back towards the forest. Her horse stumbled on uneven ground and she reeled unsteadily in the saddle. Before she could recover, Justin Douglas had seized the reins and brought her wild flight to an abrupt halt.

"Having proved how pointless it is to waste your energy in such foolishness, perhaps you will now put it to better use. We have three or four days' hard riding before us."

He sat easily on his horse watching her, and for the first time since they had met Katherine noticed a flicker of interest in his eyes. She flushed and wrapped herself in her cloak, only too aware of the tightness of the shirt she wore. A grim smile touched the corners of his mouth as if her action amused him. She was taken aback when he said:

"You ride well. In fact you ride magnificently, but if you do that again I shall tie you to the saddle. Do I make myself clear, Kate?"

"How dare you? My name is Katherine." The colour in her cheeks deepened at his insolence. No one had called her that since the death of her mother.

"I shall call you what I please. You prefer Katherine, don't you – all strait-laced and no nonsense. I prefer Kate, who if I surmise correctly has a streak of wildness in her – a desire to kick aside rules and regulations and be free. You should be able to see yourself as I see you now, with that hair loose about your shoulders, your cheeks fired with colour. You look a woman, Kate – and I must admit the change pleases me."

Floundering for words, Katherine pushed her blonde hair out of sight and held out her hand for the reins, but he shook his head and wound them securely around his saddle.

"You and I are going to stay close together from now on."

"You are enjoying this. It's a game to you, isn't it? So long as your precious King isn't caught you don't care what happens to you – or me. How many men will you have killed before this is over?"

Justin stared at her for a long moment, but his expression was unreadable and she wondered what it would take to make him lose his temper.

"More than I care to remember. Don't presume to know me, Kate – you are incapable of understanding yourself, let alone anyone else," he answered gravely, and once again she had no words to answer him.

As fast as Katherine managed to determine their position, her companion succeeded in confusing her with unexpected manoeuvres, until at last she was forced to acknowledge he had the upper hand. Throughout the day they rode continuously, making little or no attempt to conceal themselves from sight. When the food taken from the inn was gone, he stopped at a lonely farmhouse and bought bread and cheese, making sure she was seen, but not too closely. On the second day his tactics bore fruit, for they were surprised by a small troop of soldiers while resting and spent the rest of the afternoon attempting to elude them. Nightfall found them safe but exhausted, their horses unable to travel another mile. Katherine remembered being lifted from the saddle, but nothing after that until she awoke late the following morning. Justin Douglas gave her no time to deliberate on her unhappy position. Stopping only long enough to eat the last of their precious bread, they rode on.

On the fourth day they crossed a main road and Katherine saw a signpost pointing the way to Newbury.

"Are we going back?" She wheeled on her companion incredulously. "Am I to be set free now?"

"As soon as I know you can do us no harm." From the way he stared at her, Katherine knew he was finding it difficult to believe she was the same young woman he had encountered in the inn outside Bristol. She looked like an ill-shod farmer's lad instead of the daughter of one of the Lord Protector's most formidable majors, and since he had thwarted her one and only attempt to escape, she had borne his company in silence. No matter what he said or did she had not retaliated and had only looked at him with her blue eyes full of hatred and wished him dead a dozen times. Perhaps he had not expected her to put on such a courageous front.

By late afternoon they were riding over the downs above Winchester and Katherine was reeling in the saddle with tiredness. Justin halted the horses and looked down at the town stretched below them. He seemed to be trying to make up his mind about something.

"Please – can we not stop for a while?" she asked, and he turned and stared at her so intently that she felt fierce colour flood her cheeks. It was the first time she had asked any favour. He thoughtfully rubbed a hand over the growth of beard on his chin.

"I'm tired too, Kate, but I prefer to snatch some sleep out in the open. I'm not sure I can trust you to behave."

"I will do anything you ask of me. I can't go any farther." Katherine's voice broke, choked with tears, and she quickly looked away, ashamed at the display of weakness.

Untying the reins of her horse from his saddle, Justin tossed them across to her and motioned her to ride ahead.

"I have a call to make in Winchester; it will give me a chance to see how things are."

They eventually drew rein before a small jeweller's shop in a side street behind the Guildhall. Dismounting, Justin looked quickly round, helped her down and ushered her inside.

A man behind the counter was busy polishing some pieces of silver. There was no one else in the shop, but across the street Katherine could see the red and blue uniforms of

Parliamentarian soldiers. She watched them out of sight, too tired even to attempt to attract their attention.

"Can I help you, sir?" The jeweller looked up and she saw his expression widen in surprise. "Sir Justin! Are you mad, sir? The town is full of soldiers. There are more on the road to Portsmouth."

"You have the piece ready for me? You did say the 15th." Justin seemed unperturbed by the news.

"Yes – here." From beneath the counter the man brought out a long case and opened it. Carefully Justin lifted the row of pearls from its velvet bed and held it out before him.

"Martin, this is beautiful. Barbara will love it," he said, his voice full of enthusiasm. "Did it cost more than I gave you?"

"No, Sir Justin. As a matter of fact I managed to save a little."

"Then keep it, man, you've deserved it. Put them back for me. You say the town is full of soldiers?" Now he was interested – questioning.

"Two more bands of the Blue Regiment came in a few days ago," Martin the jeweller said with a distasteful grimace. "There is a dawn to dusk curfew. You must take care."

"It's almost dusk now." Justin turned and stared out of the window, uttering a soft expletive. "It seems you will have your wish, Kate. Tonight you shall sleep in a bed."

"Not here in town, Sir Justin, it's too dangerous."

"No, Martin. On the Alresford road there's an inn and the landlord is an old friend. We should reach it before the curfew begins. My thanks for all your trouble."

Katherine watched him put the jewel case into the pocket of his leather doublet and wondered who Barbara was. Someone very special for him to risk openly riding into the town, she decided. She could imagine someone very beautiful, probably dark-haired, dressed in satins and lace, waiting for her lover to bring her another token of his affection.

Justin's hand tightened over her arm as they came out of the shop and almost cannoned into a soldier and a woman companion passing by. It had begun to rain heavily. Katherine was soaked to the skin before they had reached their horses.

"Damnation, they are everywhere. Mount up quickly," he muttered. As she moved to obey he caught her wrist and held her fast again. "Give me your word you won't try to escape – or shout a warning."

Looking at him Katherine saw he had not lied when he said he too was tired. His face was drawn with weariness, his eyes dull from lack of sleep. His strength was almost gone.

"A truce, Kate. For tonight only."

Mutely she nodded, too weary to turn the situation to her own advantage.

The room where Katherine sat was warm and pleasant despite its smallness. She dozed in a chair before a blazing fire after being provided with an appetizing meal by the landlord. Behind her Justin Douglas still lingered at the table. He too had eaten well and was more than half way through the bottle of wine which had been provided. They had slipped through a side door as the curfew bell sounded through the still night air and, as in the jeweller's shop, her companion was greeted as a respected friend. Quietly they were ushered to an upstairs room and provided with dry clothes and other necessities to make them comfortable. Before the meal Justin washed and shaved. Katherine rinsed the grime from her face and hands, but it did little to revive her. She was bone-weary and longed to sleep.

"Here, drink this, it will warm you after that soaking." Justin stood before her holding out a goblet of wine.

She took it without a word and cautiously sipped at the sweet contents. He leaned against the fireplace, his dark eyes riveted on her face.

"It didn't happen the way you were told, Kate. John's death, I mean."

The blood drained from Katherine's cheeks as she looked up at him. In the flickering firelight his handsome features were grave, but his eyes unexpectedly kind. With a nervous gesture which did not escape him, she finished her drink and put the goblet aside. He picked it up, replenished it and handed it back to her.

"Don't you want to hear the truth? Are you afraid of what it might be?"

"I know how John died – you cut him down without quarter." Katherine's voice trembled, but she did not give way to the tumult of emotion suddenly coursing through her veins. "Fifteen men against eight. Do you deny that?"

"No, but you were misinformed – I think deliberately. The odds were against me and mine."

"Are you trying to tell me you outfought fifteen men? I don't believe you."

"Desperation gave strength to our blades and by God we were desperate, Kate. Our ranks had been broken, men were scattered in the fields and in the town. We were fleeing for our lives when a band of riders blocked our path – their number was unknown to me until you told me. In such circumstances counting the opposition never entered our heads." He stopped speaking and drank his wine. His eyes never left her face. "The encounter with the man you call John and his men in a cornfield on the edge of the town is still vividly clear in my mind. My dreams are haunted by the many faceless men I killed that day. Of the seven men riding with me, two were so badly hurt they did not survive the fight. Another three died beneath the blades of the troopers who surrounded us. Only three of us rode away, but behind us not one of the enemy was left standing. I did not know how many were dead or merely wounded and I had neither the time nor the inclination to force my men to remain behind and find out." The disbelieving expression on Katherine's face spurred him to ask: "Who told you I had ordered 'no quarter'?"

"They were almost the last words John spoke. A dying man does not lie . . . " Her voice trailed off and he leaned towards her, eyes glinting expectantly.

"Why do you hesitate? What other lies have you concocted to salve your wounded pride?" His words stung her as they were intended to. "I don't want to cause you more pain, but for my own peace of mind I want the truth. In killing this man did I destroy your life or merely deprive you of a useful tool?"

There was no reason why he should care, but Katherine

realized he did, and the knowledge shocked her. Turning away, he refilled his goblet and drank heavily. Katherine was feeling confused. He was deliberately feeding her wine in order to mellow her, she thought, and to make her more susceptible to his lies. Whatever happened she had to cling to what she knew was the truth. Or was it? John had not told her of the fight. By the time she reached his bedside, he was too weak to speak and soon afterwards lapsed into a deep coma which lasted for four days before he eventually died without another word. When the tears and the shock had subsided, it had been her father who related how he had died and who had been the cause of his death. She had sat alone at night and imagined the bloody incident a hundred times. The name of Justin Douglas imprinted itself on her brain, and by the time she set out for home again she had sworn a terrible vengeance on the stranger who had taken John from her. He had always been part of her life since childhood, and she had never had cause to think of life without him. Their love had been born of a mutual respect more than of passion, and she knew she would have made him happy. Now she had no one but her father, the very man John had provided an escape from – nowhere to go but the lonely house in Newbury where still lingered the ghost of her dead mother who would always be between them – and the very real figure of Francis Grahaeme, who was fast becoming as menacing as her father.

Justin's tall frame blocked out the brightness of the fire as he towered over her. He had discarded the leather doublet and through the front of his open shirt the gold locket swung to and fro before her eyes as he leaned towards her, demanding:

"You have not yet answered me. I gave no such order – who told you I did?"

"My – my father." She was reluctant to answer.

"Nathaniel Ashley! How that man can hate."

"How is it you know my father?"

"He was instrumental in having my own father hunted down and killed for his part in a plot to secure the escape of the late King. I wish I had had him at the end of my blade that day."

"Have you no shame? How easily you speak of taking a human life!" Katherine leapt to her feet, heedless of the wine spilling onto her shirt. Justin swore angrily and caught her by the shoulders, pulling her against him until his face was almost touching hers.

"Are you so different, mistress? You lied and tricked your way into the King's confidence just to have me captured. I know the bitterness personal revenge can bring . . . how it can eat at your heart and soul and finally consume you. Don't let it happen to you, Kate, you are too young."

"It already has." Katherine threw back her head and stared up into his dark features. She heard him catch his breath as the firelight struck her face. She did not know how proud and beautiful she looked – how untouchable. Slowly he shook his head.

"No, Kate. I understand your hatred but it is not as strong as you believe. Let it go now before it is too late."

"I hate you more than any other living person on this earth." Katherine spat the words at him. She could feel herself beginning to shake, but it was not because she loathed him. She was afraid of him – of the intense way he looked at her – and of his touch. That most of all. She could feel the steady beat of his heart, feel the hardness of his body against hers – hard and unyielding like the man himself, so totally different from John. It had to be the wine, she thought with rising panic. His face was so close that she was seized with the wild idea he was about to kiss her and said quickly: "Your prisoner I may be, but do not for one moment presume my morals are as loose as your own, or those of the women you associate with. Let me go this instant or I will scream."

Justin's hands fell away from her so quickly she almost lost her balance. She stepped back, away from the contempt in his expression.

"You have a high opinion of yourself. Are you jealous of Barbara by any chance? If I bought you a pretty trinket, Kate, would you be more amiable then, or do you prefer the arms of your Roundhead captain? I noticed how much you enjoyed his kisses."

Katherine's hand flashed out towards his face, but he knocked it aside.

"You begin to bore me – go to bed!" he said curtly and, seating himself in the chair she had vacated, ignored her.

Stumbling over to the bed Katherine fell across it, burying her face in the pillows to hide the tears spilling down over her cheeks. If he heard her sobs he made no comment and did not move from where he sat. It was not long before the softness of the bed relaxed her aching limbs and she gave way to the sleep which claimed her.

She was roused into wakefulness by a determined knocking on the door. Justin's hand was on his pistol as he eased it open to admit the landlord.

"Shall I clear away, Sir Justin?"

"Yes, Daniel. It was a fine meal. I see you managed to keep a few bottles of wine from the Lord Protector's men," Justin replied. If he noticed Katherine stirring, he did not show it.

"As if they would appreciate a vintage wine. They only want ale and plenty of it." Daniel Oldenshaw looked curiously towards the bed and the dishevelled girl there, but kept his questions in check.

"How does she pass as a substitute?" Justin asked with a tight smile. He leaned back against the table, arms folded over his broad chest.

"I was afraid that was your intention, in which case I think I should warn you. There was a man here when you arrived. I never gave him a second glance until you were going upstairs and I saw him watching you. He asked who you were and where you had come from. When I said I knew nothing about you he went outside and inspected your horses. I fear he may be an informer."

"Is he still here?"

"In his room. I've made sure of that."

Justin turned and stared across at Katherine, and she saw in his face a desire to leave, but to her surprise he did not order her to get up, obviously realizing she was still too tired to stay in the saddle.

"Watch him, Daniel. If he attempts to leave, let me know.

And saddle our horses just in case we have to leave in a hurry."

After the landlord had gone, Justin bolted the door and settled down in the chair again. Katherine closed her eyes, but finding it impossible to go back to sleep lay watching him from beneath lowered lids. He would doze for odd moments and then awaken and sit tense and alert for several minutes as if to satisfy himself there were no suspicious sounds, before allowing himself to relax again. She wondered how often he had slept this way since Worcester.

The first knock on the door some hours later brought him to his feet, pistol in hand. After the second knock, obviously a prearranged signal, he went quickly to unlock the door. In the light of the candle he held, Daniel Oldenshaw's face was streaked with blood and he was swaying. Justin's outstretched hand steadied him and drew him into the room.

"What happened, man? Have you been in a fight?"

"Aye – in the stables. I was saddling your horses when that man appeared. It's as I feared – he's a paid informer and probably half way to Winchester by now. I followed him outside, but when he saw me he struck me down. You must leave at once."

"Sit down before you fall." Justin guided him to a chair despite his protests. "How will you explain this to the soldiers?"

"Don't worry about me, sir. By the time they arrive I will have invented some story to tell them. Think only of yourself. If your plan, whatever it is, is to succeed, your companion must not be seen too closely, let alone caught. Hurry, the horses are waiting below."

"Thanks, old friend. I won't forget your help this night." Justin wheeled on Katherine to find her fully awake and sitting up on the bed. Knowing argument was useless, she did not protest when he pulled her to her feet and arranged her cloak over her head and shoulders. She was hurried downstairs and out into the courtyard.

"Where do we go now?"

"Don't talk – ride," Justin ordered.

When she made no move to comply, he grabbed the reins

of her horse and started off. The night air quickly revived Katherine. She became aware of the set hardness of his face, of the continual way he looked back over his shoulder as they rode, and then gradually she heard the sound of drumming hooves behind them. No sooner had she realized what it meant than Justin turned off the road and headed across country. She jerked at her reins but he wrenched them from her grasp, cursing as his action almost pulled her from the saddle. She held tight to the pommel and prayed the soldiers would overtake them. The clever King's Shadow had been careless and someone had probably recognized him. Somehow the knowledge did not bring her the satisfaction she knew it should.

In the darkness she had no idea in which direction they were heading. She guessed it was away from the town, probably through the woods where they had been only the previous day, and not long afterwards her suspicions were proved correct as they rode into a thickly wooded area. A hanging branch hit her in the face and caught at the hood covering her head. She reeled in the saddle with a cry of pain that made Justin rein in. He dragged her hood free, but it ripped and her hair spilled out over her shoulders. His fingers touched her bruised cheek and came away with blood on them. Without a word he dismounted and lifted her down. Holding her fast by the wrist he sent the horses careering off at a wild gallop, waited a moment to listen for their pursuers, and then struck off into the undergrowth. He meant the soldiers to follow a false trail, leaving them free to double back to another place of safety, she realized, and her steps lagged. Justin spun round on her and said in a curt whisper:

"No false heroics, Kate."

In answer she bent and fastened her teeth in the hand which coupled her wrist. He muttered a savage oath under his breath, wound a fistful of loose hair around his free hand and ruthlessly pulled back her head. She was forced to the ground and held there with his knee against her back while he fumbled in his pockets and produced a kerchief which he secured tightly around her mouth. She tried to scratch him and kick at his legs, but with each movement he only increased the agonizing pressure on her hair. The sound of horses and men crashing through the undergrowth grew nearer. Justin threw himself over her, the weight of his body holding her fast and almost stifling her. Wide-eyed, she stared at the sword blade only an inch or so away from her face. Outnumbered and without a mount he was still prepared to fight. He was insane!

The riders passed so close that Katherine and Justin were showered with dirt, and bits of broken brambles entwined themselves in their clothes and hair. It seemed an eternity before Justin raised his head and said quietly:

"They've gone. We can continue now."

He eased the gag from her mouth, and immediately she was on the defensive.

"And if I refuse?"

In the bright moonlight, his smile mocked her show of bravery.

"You tried that once before. One more attempt and I'll drag you by the hair." He tugged sharply at her golden tresses and she moaned in pain.

"Don't! I'll come with you."

"It will be light soon, but within three or four hours we will be at the house and then you'll be able to attend to those scratches."

Katherine brushed away the fingers reaching out to touch her cheek.

"I don't want your sympathy," she said scornfully.

"What do you want, Kate? From a man, I mean? Affection – security – love?"

"What would you know of any of those things?"

"Women usually yearn for security; a few crave affection; very rarely will a woman settle for love alone!"

Katherine sat up, turning her face away, but he spun her round, his hands clamping down over her slender shoulders. There was no escaping his grasp. Once again she began to feel panic.

"Why do you torment me so? I loved John – I was going to marry him."

Justin ignored the plea in her voice, and when she began to struggle he shook her until she became still again.

"How did you love him? With passion – like this?"

His mouth was on hers, robbing her of speech, and beneath the fierceness of his kisses her stiff lips parted and gave way. She fell back onto the ground, fighting him the only way left open to her, with the immobility of her body – a stubborn refusal to surrender to the strange feeling stealing through her, threatening to destroy everything she professed to be true. She had loved John, but he had never held her so possessively or kissed her with such depth of feeling.

When Justin drew back from her, she lay with eyes closed, feeling as if the earth was spinning in circles about her.

"I think I have proved my point," he said. Had she not been so upset, she might have heard the unsteady note in his voice. Picking up his sword, he stood up and replaced it in its scabbard. After a moment Katherine scrambled to her feet and, turning her back on him, plaited her hair and tucked it out of sight beneath the torn hood, with hands that trembled visibly.

"Kate . . . " He laid a hand on her arm, suddenly contrite. She flinched away from him as if his touch was scalding hot, and opened her mouth to heap insults on his head, but none were uttered. He stepped closer, warning her to silence as from somewhere in the darkness beyond came the sound of movement.

"A soldier?" Katherine whispered, and her hopes rose again.

"Perhaps – or a poacher – even an animal."

He stepped away from her, drawing the pistol from his belt. Katherine's eyes gleamed as they fastened on it. The sound of a shot would carry for miles – the soldiers would hear it and return. It was a desperate gamble, but one she was willing to take. The pistol turned to menace her as she moved backwards.

"Be still!" Justin hissed.

"You dare not shoot me. I am no use to you dead," she challenged, "and the sound of a shot will bring the soldiers back."

She saw the indecision which crossed his face and knew she

was right. She turned and ran through the bushes, towards whoever or whatever lay in the darkness ahead.

He was several yards behind her when she came upon a soldier leading the lame horse that had separated him from the rest of the troop. Without thinking, she called out and began to run towards him.

"Katherine – no!" She heard Justin's desperate call, but ignored it, not realizing the danger she was in. The trooper saw not a frightened girl, but a young man in a cloak who closely fitted the description of the fugitive King he had earlier been chasing. He had been cursing his ill luck and now it had suddenly changed. Justin came out of the trees to one side of Katherine as the man lifted his musket and took careful aim, lifted his pistol and fired.

Both weapons exploded simultaneously. Katherine screamed as a burning pain seared one side of her head. She toppled forward onto a patch of ferns and moss and knew no more.

CHAPTER FOUR

KATHERINE'S return to consciousness was slow and painful. The figure bending over her was not clearly visible for some time, then gradually as the mists before her eyes cleared she was able to make out the features of Justin Douglas.

"Thank God, you are all right. I was beginning to think . . ." Sitting back on his heels, he produced a silver flask from his doublet and put it to her lips, supporting her head with one hand. "Drink a little of this . . . slowly now."

Katherine coughed as the neat brandy burned her throat. She had never taken spirits in her life before, and not only the taste but the smell revolted her, and she made a feeble attempt to push him away. An agonizing pain shot through her temples and she lay back in the crook of his arm with a soft moan, unprotesting as he put the flask to her lips again and forced her to swallow another mouthful.

"Now lie still and try to sleep. Are you cold? It was raining again when I found this place."

Katherine realized she was wrapped in his cloak. It was dry. Her own was spread in front of the fire burning a few feet away. They appeared to be in some kind of barn. To one side of her were bales of hay and an old cart. Two pieces of sacking were hung across the window embrasures.

"No – I – I feel very dizzy, but warm."

"That's the brandy. What luck I brought it with me. When it gets dark I'll steal a horse and then we can be on our way again at first light. My home is less than five miles from here. Rest, Kate. Tomorrow you will sleep in a soft bed."

"The soldiers," Katherine murmured dazedly. Her memory was returning . . . she recalled those last few minutes when she had faced the trooper, rooted to the spot with fear as he levelled his musket at her in the belief she was the King in disguise. And Justin's warning . . . why had she not listened?"

"You tried to warn me . . . thank you." The words did not come easily to her lips and she saw him smile in the shadowy light. "Why don't you leave me here? Someone will find me before too long. I can do you no harm now."

"You know where the King is hiding, so you are still dangerous to me, Kate. No, I cannot let you go yet, but I will soon – I promise. Until then why don't we extend our truce?" His hand lightly smoothed back some loose hair over her forehead. She winced as his fingers touched the wound at the side of her head, and he abruptly drew back. Katherine's eyes closed – she felt exhausted.

"Anything . . . only let me sleep . . . please."

Katherine slept for several hours. When she awoke her clothes were clinging to her body, which was wet with perspiration. She pushed away the cloak covering her, but moments later Justin rearranged it around her, talking in quiet tones to her as he wiped her wet forehead.

"Not long now, Kate. Try to rest."

When she opened her eyes again, he was scattering earth onto the fire. It was growing late. Time for them to be moving again.

"How do you feel?" He bent over her, his dark eyes scrutinizing her face. Before she could move her hand away, he laid cool fingers against her wrist. She shivered beneath his touch. How she hated feeling so weak and wretched. It forced her to be reliant on his strength. She preferred him to be rude and arrogant, making it easier to continue hating him.

"I can manage quite well alone." She ignored the outstretched hand intended to help her and tried to sit up by herself. The effort brought a cry of pain to her lips.

"No, I thought you could not. My poor, foolish Kate – so proud." Carefully Justin wrapped her in her own cloak which was now dry and warm and lifted her from the ground. Her cheek lay against the cold leather of his doublet as he carried her out to the horse tethered by the open door. She realized he had left her while she slept to steal it. The gentleness with which he settled her before him on the saddle and watched over her during the next few hours hardly penetrated her dulled senses. She lay against him almost insensible, seeing nothing of the countryside through which they passed, unaware of the jerking motions of the horse. She felt as if she was in a dream world, full of shadows, where nothing was real. She fancied Justin kissed her lightly on the cheek – just once – but of course she could not be sure.

The sun was warm on her face. She stirred and pushed away the rough material around her shoulders, suddenly aware that Justin had reined in. They were on the brow of a hill. Below them was a palatial mansion. Tall green poplars on two sides were a perfect setting for the elegantly designed building built completely of white stone. Beautifully laid out gardens sloped down to a lake which shimmered in the early morning sunlight.

"Look, Kate. My home," Justin said quietly.

The deep pleasure in his voice told her how much he loved this place. Skirting the house in a wide circle, he approached from the rear. It looked deserted. Katherine wondered if it was under surveillance from the distant trees, knew by the tenseness in Justin's face as he dismounted that he was pondering the same thought. He carried her to the edge of the stone-flagged path leading across the lawn. His single piercing whistle was not answered. She guessed it was some kind of prearranged signal, for in a moment or two he repeated it. Almost immediately the french windows opened and Simon Douglas appeared, beckoning. With Katherine in his arms, Justin strode swiftly across the open space and into the drawing-room where his brother stood.

"No questions. She's hurt and in need of attention," he said brusquely as his brother looked questioningly at Katherine. "Where is Mother?"

"Here, Justin."

Katherine's vision was so blurred by this time that she could not put a face to the very quiet, soothing voice.

"What happened to the poor girl?"

"She was shot by a trooper."

"I will attend to her myself. We cannot risk having a doctor here. Simon, go and find your sister, I shall need some of her clothes. Justin, bring your charge upstairs. She shall have a room near mine in the west wing."

Katherine was vaguely aware of a long, wide staircase, carpeted corridors and walls covered with tapestries and paintings, before she was gently deposited on a comfortable four-poster bed. Beneath her aching head the pillow felt as soft as gossamer, and she had to fight off the drowsiness creeping into her limbs.

"Justin!" A pretty, brown-haired girl came through the doorway and flung herself into the arms of Justin Douglas. "Oh, I've been so worried. It's been so long . . . are you hurt?"

He held her close against him, his face buried in her thick hair. When he drew back he was smiling.

"Hurt? I haven't met a Roundhead yet who can catch me, let alone engage me in a fight."

"Don't joke, we all know how bad it was at Worcester – and afterwards. That awful woman almost had you caught." The girl was looking towards the bed, her expression full of malice. "Simon said you made her dress as a boy and pretend to be the King. I hope you gave her a hard time. Oh! You are hurting me!"

Justin's hands were clenched tightly on her shoulders and his face was a bleak mask. Abruptly he released her and stepped to one side, allowing her to see Katherine's dishevelled condition and terrible pallor.

"Because of what I made her do, this awful woman, as you call her, has been injured. She could have been killed. You judge too harshly, Barbara, and too quickly. She had good reason for what she did to us."

"For betraying you to your death?" his mother said quietly. "What is it we do not know?"

"I helped to kill her man at Worcester – perhaps it was even my blade which cut him down." Katherine watched a tiny nerve throbbing at his temple as he answered, but almost immediately her eyes went back to where the young girl stood. So this was Barbara – the person for whom he had risked capture in order to buy her pearl necklace.

"Many men die in battle. You cannot blame yourself for what happened and she has no right to hold you responsible," Justin's mother replied.

"I'm too tired to argue. Will you care for her?"

"Of course."

"You can't," Barbara protested. "She almost had them all killed. Why should we help her?"

"Because Justin asks it of us. Where is her maid?"

"Still locked in the servants' quarters. Simon seems to have taken personal charge of her."

Katherine could have cried with relief at the news. Sarah was safe and not far away. It would be good to have a friend again.

"Have her brought here. I want clean towels and hot water, and you had better bring me some of your night clothes."

"Thank you," Justin said as Barbara left the room. The relief in his voice was not lost on Katherine. He was glad to get his unwanted burden off his hands.

"Does she have a name?"

"Kate – Katherine." Justin gave Katherine no chance to answer herself. "I must speak with the King and then go to bed. Tell Simon to keep a watch at all times and wake me if there is any trouble."

"A guard has already been posted. Go to bed, my son. You can do no more here."

Katherine watched his tall figure disappear through the door and then she relaxed and allowed her eyes to close. All she wanted to do was sleep and awaken without the terrible pain in her head.

The following morning she awoke from the deep sleep which had claimed her for over twelve hours. Apart from a slight headache, which was nowhere as bad as the one she had previously endured, and a few bruises, she found she was none the worse for her frightening experience. She opened her eyes onto a large, comfortably furnished room, with a thick brightly-patterned carpet on the floor and heavy velvet curtains at the windows. The four-poster bed where she lay was hung with pretty pink drapes to match the counterpane and the rest of the very pleasant décor. A faint flush stole into her cheeks as she stared down at the nightdress she wore and touched the delicate material. How different it was from the cotton gowns she wore at home, and how much more pleasant. As a child, her love of pretty things had often brought severe chastisement from her father. He was a hard man with no understanding of a woman's needs. He would destroy her life as surely as he had her mother's – and her one chance of escape had died with John at Worcester.

How strange, she thought, that it should have taken a brush with death to make her accept the truth. Her marriage and the new life it offered would have meant freedom from her father's domination and a chance to do all the things he had never allowed. Justin Douglas – or one of his men – had deprived her of that chance, and for that she would never forgive him. No matter what her reasons were for wanting to marry John – or whether the account given to her by her father of the fight in which he died was true or not – Justin had still taken from her a chance to live and not merely exist.

She tried to sit up, but her head was too painful and she lay back with a sigh. She was at Justin's home, among people who were totally alien to her and her way of life, and Charles was here too, so close and yet so far from capture. With the capable King's Shadow always at hand, she was beginning to wonder if he would ever be taken. His escape to France would mean his able bodyguard would also go free and John's death would remain unpunished. She had fought hard to avert such a situation, but now she was here as a prisoner in the Douglas house, with no chance of seeing her plans realized.

Closing her eyes she tried to sleep again, but instead she found her mind dwelling on those few moments in the wood before she had run in panic from the man who had held her helpless in his arms and shown her how good it felt to be a woman. She knew that in that short time she had learned more about herself than in all the years she might have spent with

John. The knowledge did not make her feel very proud of herself.

She liked Elizabeth Douglas, Justin's mother, from the moment the woman came into the room and introduced herself. The quiet voice and friendly smile, the warmth in the blue eyes which surveyed her, all helped to put Katherine at her ease, making it easy to forget that this attractive woman who tended her so painstakingly was the mother of the man she hated.

"You are looking much better this morning, my dear." Elizabeth sat in a chair beside the bed and watched her eating the breakfast Sarah had brought.

"I feel a fraud," Katherine confessed. "I am really quite well now."

"Then you can get up for a while if you wish. I'll ask my daughter to find something for you to wear."

"You are being very kind to me. I think it only fair to tell you who I am," Katherine began, but Elizabeth Douglas held up her hand.

"Your name is Katherine and you are the daughter of Nathaniel Ashley, the man who hunted down and killed my husband. Justin has told me all about you. Unlike you, my dear, I have learned it is better not to hunger after revenge. It is bad for the soul. I see no reason why we cannot be friends, despite our differences."

Katherine finished her tray and immediately Sarah came to take it away.

"Go and find my daughter and tell her our guest is in need of something pretty to wear," Elizabeth ordered her and then turned back to Katherine. "You must stay with us until you are quite well."

Katherine smiled faintly. Yes, she would be staying – Justin would make sure of that. She was too dangerous to be set free.

"I am well – really I am. Thank you for your kind offer, but I am afraid there will be trouble if I remain here." How nice it would have been to accept the well-meant offer.

"Inconvenience perhaps, if the house is searched again, but not trouble. We will think of some reason for your being here."

"If the soldiers come I will tell them the King is here – I must, it is my duty and that would mean trouble for you. You must make Sir Justin let me go before that happens." When the woman did not answer Katherine felt her heartbeats quicken. "You cannot do that, can you? I am a prisoner – his prisoner, not your guest as you want me to believe."

"No, my dear, you are my guest," Elizabeth assured her. "This is my house and here even Justin obeys me. I have told him I will not have you treated like a prisoner. You are, of course, his responsibility with so much at stake, but while you are beneath my roof, I will treat you no differently from my own family."

"I – I don't understand you," Katherine said faintly. "Sir Justin himself told me about your husband. You should hate me for what my father did."

"Hate is a destructive emotion. I understand why you set out to attempt such a dangerous mission, but I don't condone it. You are very brave, but at the same time foolish, and I think it is now time to forget all that has happened." Elizabeth stood up, her blue eyes thoughtful as they stared into the pale face of the girl before her. Obviously Katherine's presence in the house was more disturbing than she would admit. "When you are dressed, ask Barbara to show you the gardens. The peace and serenity of a pretty flower garden is soothing to a troubled mind."

As the door closed behind Elizabeth Douglas, Katherine fell back onto the pillows, her mind reeling. The girl who had embraced Justin so warmly was his sister Barbara – not his mistress. The ugly picture of him she had conjured up in her mind, prompted by the purchase of the pearls and the gold locket he wore about his neck, was wiped out by this new revelation. However, there was still the possibility of a woman in his life, and why should there not be? He was attractive and courageous and, when he chose to be, utterly charming. Katherine put both hands against her burning cheeks. She was mad to think of him in such a fashion – they were worlds apart and the gap between them could never be closed.

The door opened again and Sarah came in carrying several

pairs of shoes and underclothes, and behind her another girl whose arms were full of dresses.

"Good morning. I'm Justin's sister Barbara." She dropped the clothes at the end of the bed and smiled at Katherine. She was small, but dark like her brother. Her long hair was curled in ringlets about her shoulders and tied back with a ribbon matching the yellow dress she wore.

"I'm Katherine."

"Yes, I know. Simon told us all about you before Justin ever brought you here."

"All?"

"I admit I didn't like you very much at first, Katherine Ashley, but now I think I understand. In your place I might have acted the same way."

"I'm not ashamed of what I did. I – I would do it again," Katherine declared, and almost succeeded in convincing herself it was the truth.

"Because of what happened at Worcester? You can't blame Justin for that. My father died at the hands of the Roundheads, but what good will it do me to blame them? It won't bring him back, will it?"

"I wish I could feel that way, but I can't."

Barbara regarded her seriously for a moment and in silence they took each other's measure, then she turned and took the undergarments Sarah held and spread them out over the bed.

"You must choose whatever you want. My mother is waiting to see you in the garden."

As Katherine stood up, a wave of dizziness swept over her and she swayed on her feet. Immediately Sarah was at her side to steady her, and all hostility vanished from Barbara's face at the sight of the sudden pallor in Katherine's cheeks.

"Are you all right? Quickly, Sarah, some water. Sit down, Katherine, until the faintness passes. Did I upset you? I'm sorry to sound so harsh, but Justin is my brother and I love him. He is a wonderful man, incapable of killing anyone in cold blood. You believe him to be some kind of heartless monster, but he isn't . . . if he was, would he have risked so much to bring you here? He could have left you injured and alone out there in the woods."

That was something Katherine had already wondered about. Why had he burdened himself with her when he could have left her for the soldiers to find? It could have been hours, even days, before she was discovered, and by then he could have snatched the King to safety and vanished again. Instead he had cared for her throughout the night and brought her to his home. She did not understand his actions, and it made her even more beholden to these people who had taken her in and cared for her.

"I wish he had," she said at length. "I am so afraid my presence here will cause trouble for you and your mother, and I do not want that to happen. You have both been very kind to me – "

"Nonsense!" Barbara interrupted, and Katherine saw her blush. "Now, which dress do you prefer – the green or the pink?"

The reflection which stared back at her from the ornamental mirror was not that of Katherine Ashley, but of an elegant woman who possessed both poise and confidence. Was the silk dress she wore the only reason for such a transformation, Katherine wondered, or had the events of the past weeks opened her eyes to more than the narrow world in which she had existed for so long? If only her father could see her now, admiring the attributes she had possessed for many years, but had never been allowed to acknowledge – the trim waist and softly rounded breasts, enhanced by the perfect cut of the gown . . . the creamy whiteness of her shoulders and arms. Barbara had insisted on dressing her hair and had brushed it back behind her ears, secured it with pins and twisted the blonde strands into long curls to fall about her shoulders.

Voices floated up to her through the open window. Cautiously she stood behind a curtain and looked down on Elizabeth Douglas and the King as they walked in the garden. She was expected to join them as if she was an honoured guest instead of a prisoner. She did not belong with the Douglas family, nor did she want them to be nice to her. She did not belong in this huge sprawling house where she was finding it increasingly difficult to keep her thoughts in context. How she longed for the sanctuary of her own home where it was so easy to remember who and what she was! How she despised the weakness in her which rebelled against taking off the pink dress and returning to bed and staying there until she was allowed to go free. Yet despise it as she did, she submitted to it and went downstairs.

"Well, I'm damned!" Charles ejaculated as she appeared before them on the path. Without a word Katherine curtsied low before him, aware of the startled look on the face of Elizabeth Douglas as he raised her fingers to his lips and bade her rise. "Your manners have improved, Mistress Ashley. Clothes do make a lady after all."

Katherine flushed at his sarcasm, but did not retaliate, knowing it was fully deserved.

"I have no excuse for my earlier rudeness to Your Majesty, nor for my behaviour. You must deal with me as you see fit," she said with great dignity.

"No, that is Justin's prerogative. I have granted his request that you remain solely in his charge." Katherine's hand, still in his, began to tremble and was quickly withdrawn. Charles gave her a friendly smile. "I think if Mistress Ashley gives us her word of honour that she will remain here peaceably, we should accept it, don't you?" he asked, turning to Lady Douglas.

"Why, yes – of course." Elizabeth Douglas was still staring at Katherine, obviously finding it difficult to reconcile this well-groomed figure with the girl her son had brought to the house.

"Well?" Charles turned back to Katherine. "Do you agree? It would make things so much more pleasant for us all."

"You have my word." She did not hesitate with her answer. What other choice was open to her?

"Good. Now I suggest you ask Simon, who is hovering a few feet behind you, to show you these most delightful grounds. I must go inside again; I have lingered out here longer than is advisable. Will you join us later for a glass of wine?"

"As Your Majesty pleases." Katherine curtsied again as he passed, and when she rose he was moving towards the house with Elizabeth Douglas on his arm and Simon was at her side, open admiration in his eyes.

"You – look different."

"It is only the dress, I assure you," Katherine said, turning away. This was Justin's brother, also her enemy. She wondered if they had discussed her. "You don't have to stay with me. I have given the King my word and I won't break it."

"I believe you, but I want to stay – if you don't mind. How is your head today?"

"It feels twice the size it should be. I was lucky, wasn't I?"

"Yes. Justin said if the wound had been a trifle more to the left . . . but it was not, so we won't dwell on it."

"Thank you for caring for Sarah. She has been treated well. I was afraid . . . "

"That I might seduce her?" Simon mocked gently, and she flushed.

"She is very young," she said, in defence of her suspicions.

"And very sweet. I have grown quite fond of her."

"Did you have any trouble coming here?"

"None, thanks to Justin's ingenious idea. We were only stopped once and the trooper in charge was a most obliging fellow. I wish you had fared as well, Mistress Katherine."

"Surely it is dangerous for you to remain so close to Winchester – the town is full of soldiers, with still more regiments arriving."

"The house was searched a few hours before we arrived. I suspect they intend to spread a wide net for us, in which case we will be safer here for a while. We have a man posted on the high ground. From there he can see for miles and we shall have at least half an hour's warning if anyone comes in this direction. Within less time we can obliterate any traces of our being here and then escape through the tunnel."

So there was another way to freedom, Katherine thought. She should have known Justin Douglas would not unnecessarily risk the life of his royal master.

They walked back along the path and across the lawn into a

group of trees on the far side. Katherine was back in her dream world again, but this time instead of the pain and shadow there was the warmth of the sun on her face and the touch of silk against her skin. For a while she was being allowed luxuries her father had always denied her – beautiful clothes – the company of people other than those he chose himself – a chance to see and learn about another way of life.

"You are very quiet," Simon remarked as she paused to look back at the house.

"I was thinking how lucky you are to live here and to have such a wonderful mother and sister."

"Sarah told me your mother is dead – I'm sorry. What was she like?"

"A very shy woman and frightened of my father."

"I think you are too," Simon said with a frown. "That isn't a good thing."

Katherine considered the possibility for a long moment before nodding her head.

"Yes, I suppose I am. He is a hard man. Perhaps if I had been a boy he might have loved me."

"Was John to have taken the place of the son he never had?"

Katherine looked at him sharply, but his smile disarmed her.

"No, John was too gentle. They didn't get on too well together. Father liked him, but always considered him too soft. He might have survived if he had been harder and more ruthless. Father preferred John's brother Francis. You saw him at the inn."

"Many men died at Worcester," Simon reminded her. "Single men – family men with wives and children to go back to. In war there's no time to ask a man if he's hard or soft, good or bad, especially when his blade is aimed at your heart."

"Are you trying to justify what your brother did?"

"I don't think I have to – I just want you to realize what it was like that day. Sarah tells me you were told it was a cold-blooded massacre – that isn't true. I know, because I was there too. We were outnumbered by more than two to one. Despera-tion gave us strength and that's God's solemn truth."

Katherine was silent. She had grown very pale and her

hands were clenched nervously by her sides. Everything inside her cried out that she should believe him, but to do so would also mean she must accept John's death as a cruel fact of war and lay no blame on the shoulders of Justin Douglas. To do this would mean that everything she had suffered at his hands had been brought about by her own selfish desire for revenge.

She was saved from committing herself, for at that moment a rider came galloping through the trees ahead of them and drew rein beside them. Katherine found herself staring up into Justin's cold, angry features.

"What the devil are you doing out here?" he demanded harshly.

"The King has her word of honour not to escape," Simon said, stepping forward. He touched the horse's flank and exclaimed softly: "You've been riding hard – is anything wrong?"

"Nothing. I just wanted to get something out of my system, that's all," came the terse reply. "I suggest you take Mistress Ashley back to the house. I am not so ready to accept her word as you are." He scarcely glanced at Katherine's general appearance. His eyes were riveted on her face, dark with suspicion.

"Justin, that's not fair," his brother protested, darting a look at Katherine's dismayed features.

"Take her back – or must I do it?"

"I can manage perfectly well alone," Katherine declared. Picking up her skirts and turning away, she hurried back towards the house, wanting desperately to run, but knowing if she did he would realize how deeply his cruel words had hurt her.

CHAPTER FIVE

As Katherine saw Justin Douglas and Simon coming across the lawn, she excused herself from the King's company and hurried towards the stairs, but before she had reached them she met Barbara, who came flying out of the music-room as if chased by a thousand demons.

"Isn't it wonderful! Look at my birthday present!" she said gaily, waving a string of pearls before her. Katherine needed only one look to realize it was the one which Justin had purchased in Winchester.

"Yes, they are very nice. You didn't tell me it was your birthday."

"It isn't until tomorrow. I want a party, but Justin insists it is too dangerous."

"Nonsense! The relaxation would do us all good," Charles declared, advancing from the doorway behind them. "May I see those exquisite pearls? Beautiful! Justin has a good eye. You must wear them tomorrow, together with your prettiest gown. It has been a long time since I have had the choice of so many attractive dancing partners. You will join us, of course, Mistress Ashley."

Justin entered through the french windows, and as he came towards them the sight of him determined her answer.

"No, sire, I must refuse. I am not a good dancer, and besides, my presence would strike a somewhat sour note in the celebrations. May I have your leave to go to my room?"

"No, you may not." Charles frowned with annoyance and spun round on Justin. "Mistress Ashley wishes to deprive me of her company – you must rectify that for me."

"She will be better out of it, sire, and once again I must insist you reconsider this idea."

"Justin, my dear fellow, why don't you relax for a few hours? I am soon going into exile, far from my friends. I want to take with me as many happy memories as I can. We shall have ample warning if the troopers return this way. I will hear no more against it. I want Barbara to have her party and Mistress Ashley to attend it. How you persuade her is up to you."

Katherine did not wait to hear any more. She brushed past Barbara and ran upstairs. She had not been in her room ten minutes when the door opened and Justin came in.

"May I speak with you?"

"Why not? Whatever your mother says I am still a prisoner, and if you want to talk with me then I suppose I must listen." She sat down again with her back towards him and did not look up when he came to stand beside her.

"I come from the King. It is his wish that you attend tomorrow night, not mine. He will not accept a refusal."

"Why am I so important?"

"He has his grandfather's eye for a pretty face." She felt the colour rise in her cheeks, realizing his earlier angry attitude had been caused by her appearance in one of his sister's dresses and by the way she was so readily accepted beneath his roof. And now the King was paying attention to her, to provoke him further.

"Are you quite recovered?" His tone was impersonal.

"Yes. What is to happen to me when you have taken the King elsewhere?" She looked at him for the first time since he had entered the room. He frowned as he saw the fierce red scar left by the Roundhead bullet, just visible beneath the wispy fringe brushed across her forehead.

"I haven't decided yet."

"I am no further danger to you. Why won't you let me go?"

He sprawled on the window seat beside her and stared blindly down at his leather riding boots.

"Perhaps I keep you here for purely selfish reasons."

Her startled gaze searched his face, but she looked away quickly as he raised his head, and his eyes challenged her to admit something she could not – even to herself. "Have no fear, as soon as we have gone, you will be freed. I would ask a favour of you, however. Not to implicate my mother and sister. I have no wish to see them imprisoned."

"Cromwell does not wage war on women," Katherine returned quickly. "His men would not have made me a prisoner, as you have – subjected me to insults and privations and almost had me killed."

"Would they not? I wish I had your faith. As for almost getting you killed, it would not have happened if you had stayed with me and not run off."

"I – I wanted to get away from you," Katherine stammered. "I was afraid."

He looked at her, genuinely amazed.

"Of me? Why? Because you discovered my kisses gave you pleasure?"

She jumped to her feet and would have turned away, but his hand snaked out, fastened over her wrist, holding her fast.

"One day you will learn to be honest with yourself. I hope it won't be too late for you to find happiness. Now, your promise not to involve my womenfolk. Do I have it?"

"Why should I care what happens to them?" Katherine asked coldly. She would do nothing to place them in danger, but would not give him the satisfaction of knowing how she felt. She wanted to hurt him as deeply as he had hurt her.

The fingers grasping her wrist tightened painfully, and a contemptuous smile tilted the corners of his mouth.

"Thank you for not proving me wrong, Kate."

"I don't understand you."

"There's no reason why you should. It was something Barbara said, that's all. If I don't have your promise, I may decide to take you with us."

"And jeopardize the King's safety? I doubt that. Do you think I can't guess your destination? It has to be a coastal town near a shipping lane, in order to find a vessel to take you to France."

Justin's eyes glittered at her uncontrollable outburst. Katherine could have bitten off her tongue. Each careless word made her more dangerous to him.

"To take the King, Kate. I am remaining behind."

"In England! Are you mad?"

"My family are here, and besides, I would not take kindly to the boredom of exile. But I must be sure of you. Don't make me use measures I shall regret to ensure your silence."

Katherine blanched. She glanced down at the lean brown fingers encircling her wrist and then up into his expressionless features, but she did not question him further. To him the King was all-important and she knew he would do whatever was necessary to protect him.

"I will say nothing – do nothing to endanger your mother and Barbara," she said, after a long silence had ensued between them. "I have not forgotten I owe you my life, and therefore I will keep silent as to your plans for the King. I do not wish to be indebted to you, Sir Justin. Please release me – my wrist feels as if it is about to break."

Justin let her go. The marks of his fingers were imprinted on her skin, and he frowned.

"You are a worthy adversary, Kate, but I prefer not to fight you," he said quietly. "I accept your word."

"And when you leave?"

"One of the servants will escort you safely to Newbury, or wherever you want to go. I believe you when you say you will not betray us – but if you do, I swear I will find you and you will pay dearly for it."

Katherine winced as she rubbed her bruised wrist, and he turned away as if the sight disturbed him.

"You will have to trust me, just as I must believe I shall be safely escorted from this house and not left dead in a ditch somewhere."

Justin crossed to the door and opened it. "If you play me false, no one will deprive me of the pleasure of personally choking the life out of you," he warned. "I will tell the King you are to join us tomorrow evening then?"

Katherine nodded. As the door closed behind him she fell back into a chair, trembling violently. She did not venture out of her room again that day.

She could not sleep that night. For hours she lay beneath the pink canopy, watching the moon's slow progress across the sky through the open window. Her head was throbbing madly, making it impossible to lie still and relax. The lawn nightdress she wore clung to her body as she got up, slipped into the robe lying across the bed and pushed her feet into a pair of Barbara's slippers.

The house was quiet. The tall grandfather clock outside her room registered two o'clock as she stole past to the head of the stairs. Candles still burned in the enormous wrought iron candelabra which hung in the centre of the Great Hall, illuminating the way downstairs. Sightless eyes from the family portraits hanging beside the balustrade followed Katherine's progress to the huge yawning chasm of a fireplace which stretched for at least ten feet at the other end. The Douglas coat of arms was emblazoned directly above it. She had seen it many times throughout the house – a lone hawk in flight – and beneath, the simple inscription, "Alone, but unafraid". Somehow it was symbolic of Justin Douglas. A portrait of him hung above the crest. The dark eyes considered her as she stared up at it, as disturbing on canvas as they were in reality. She could feel their compelling gaze following her as she turned and started back upstairs – so forceful that she had to turn and look back as if to reassure herself it was only her imagination.

A soft grating sound arrested her attention. It seemed to come from the direction of the fireplace. Her eyes widened as a section of the brickwork swung inwards behind the dying embers in the hearth and Justin Douglas emerged. Stepping out, he reached up and touched the wings of the hawk, and the concealed entrance closed noiselessly behind him. So this was the tunnel Simon had mentioned. Where did it lead? she wondered.

Not looking to left or right, Justin crossed the hall and went into one of the downstairs rooms. Hardly daring to breathe, Katherine crept back to the fireplace, touched the stone wings with trembling fingers and watched the hidden door swing open. One hurried glance behind to ensure she had not been seen, then she was stepping into the long, winding tunnel where wall torches burned at regular intervals along the way.

She tried to close the door, but could find no way of doing so and for a moment she hesitated. Could she risk going on?

Curiosity got the better of her. The passage widened out after a few yards and she came upon an area about ten feet by eight. It contained a small table and an oil lamp, a palliasse of straw with a pistol lying on the top, and some blankets. Instinctively she knew this was where the King would hide if enemy troopers returned to the house. Her robe dragged in inches of dirt as she cautiously moved on. After another twenty yards or so she came upon a wooden door, bolted on her side. She unlocked and opened it to find the way barred by a piece of furniture which, to her surprise, yielded to her pushing, and she stepped out from behind a small altar to find herself in the semi-darkness of a chapel. From the window she could distinctly see a clearing in the bright moonlight, with a thickly wooded area beyond. Anyone wishing to escape from the house unseen had the choice of either hiding in the tunnel, or if that became too dangerous, slipping out of the chapel and losing themselves in the trees. She was shivering as she retraced her steps, but out of cold, fear or excitement, she did not know.

As her fingers touched the hawk's cold wings and the door began to close behind her, a lean hand gripped hers and she spun round to face Justin Douglas, his features dark with suspicion.

"So, I can't trust you after all, Kate." Despite the quietness of his tone she detected the underlying anger, for the moment held in check. She knew he had seen her enter the passage and had awaited her return.

"I – I . . . " What could she say, apart from the truth? "I could not sleep . . . I saw you . . . "

"And decided to explore for yourself. Why did you come back? Are you hoping the troopers will return, enabling you to denounce the King in a style to make your father proud of you?"

"No!" The idea horrified her.

"I am in no mood to be lied to, Kate. Did you go into the chapel?"

"Yes."

His eyes grew puzzled. He could no more understand her return to the house than she could. She could have fled, found help to take her to the nearest garrison, but the idea had never occurred to her.

"I promised you I would do nothing to endanger the lives of your sister and mother. Why do you find it so difficult to believe I will keep my word?" She raised a trembling hand to her head. "Please may I go back to my room?"

The fierce grip on her relaxed, but Justin did not release her, and his expression changed to one of concern as he stared down into her face.

"That injury has taken more out of you than you realize. You are quite pale. Come into the library – I have some excellent old brandy there to warm those cold bones."

"No." Katherine hung back, suddenly aware she wore only a nightdress and robe. She had never been alone with a man in such disarray before. "I would prefer to go upstairs, Sir Justin. I am tired."

"A moment ago you could not sleep," Justin objected. "You have nothing to fear, Kate." The implication was not lost on her and she followed him without further protest.

He led her to a comfortable chair beside a table littered with open books. Her questioning eyes met his as she curled up in it, pulling the robe self-consciously around her throat, and saw his mouth curve in a smile.

"Are you surprised I like to read, Kate? I assure you I prefer a book in my hand to a sword."

"I find that hard to believe. You have a natural talent for the life you lead. You enjoy it," Katherine challenged.

Placing a decanter and two glasses on the table between them, Justin pulled up another chair and relaxed into it with a grimace.

"I don't deny there are times when I do, but those are few and far between."

"How will you live when you are in France, without money or position to aid you?"

"I will do whatever is necessary to survive, should the

occasion arise, but as I have already told you, I am remaining behind," he returned calmly, pouring brandy into the two delicately engraved crystal glasses. Katherine took hers and sipped the contents with some reserve, remembering how it had burned her throat once before, but this brandy was totally different; it was smooth and mellow and slid down without effort.

"You mean you would sell your sword – become a mercenary?"

"Yes, I do mean that. Why should the thought disturb you? You will be safe at home under your father's loving wing, probably being courted by Captain Grahaeme. If that is what you want, then I wish you well."

Katherine lowered her gaze, wishing he had not reminded her of Francis and the prospect of his constant presence in the house now he was quartered there. It was not what she wanted, but she could not tell him so.

"You may go where you wish and do whatever takes your fancy, Sir Justin," she said, a trifle sharply. "It is of no interest to me. I was thinking of how your absence might affect your family."

"My mother has survived many hardships in the past and Barbara is fast growing to be like her. They know I will not leave unless there is no other choice, in which case they will manage until I return."

"It would be your intention to return in the end?"

"England is my home, Kate – I could not bear to leave it for ever," came the quiet reply, and she was stirred by the sincerity in his voice. "I don't want to be parted from this house where I was born, from a mother and a sister I adore – from – " He broke off, frowning down at his glass. From what? Katherine wondered – or whom? But he did not continue.

Replenishing his glass, he leaned across and refilled hers. His dark features were unexpectedly solemn as he sat drinking in silence, and Katherine said nothing to disturb his thoughts. The brandy had warmed and relaxed her exactly as the wine had done the night they had sought shelter in the inn at Alresford. Bitter words had passed between them then when she had refused to believe he had not helped to kill John in cold blood. It was easier to accept it as the truth now, although part of her still fought against it, condemning her for even wanting to take the word of a man whose way of life was so totally alien to hers and everything she had ever been taught to believe in. Good and evil – it was hard to distinguish between them sometimes. Cromwell against Charles – her father against Justin Douglas. Only God had the right to determine who should be victorious.

"I will say nothing about the tunnel," Katherine said, suddenly raising her head. "Even after I am home. I swear it."

"Are you so afraid of me, Kate?" His question disturbed her. It was as if he could see into her very soul – read her every thought. Yes, she was afraid, but not in the way he meant. Something had happened to her in the short time she had been in his house. No, if she was honest with herself, it had all begun the very first time he looked at her. Nothing had been the same, or would be again. He looked at her as if he was aware of something of which she was not . . . "The colour is coming back to your cheeks. Good." Justin gave a nod of satisfaction. His eyes surveyed her for a long moment, dwelling on the loose hair cascading down over her shoulders, then abruptly he stood up as if her presence was suddenly disturbing to him. "I think perhaps you should return to your bed now."

He escorted her back to her room and left her at the door. Katherine climbed back into bed puzzled by the curt dismissal.

She remained in her room the next day despite the sounds of revelry which floated up to her from the gardens, tempting her to go down. Barbara and Simon were there, laughing together beneath the arbour. As she watched them from the window, Justin joined them and she drew back out of sight lest he looked up and saw her. He was casually dressed in a pair of breeches and a white shirt, open almost to the waist. He stood on the path, his arms folded, a smile on his face as he talked with his brother and sister. There was a knife in the leather sheath attached to the wide belt around his waist. She had noticed he never went anywhere without a weapon of some kind, even in the house. Elizabeth Douglas walked across the lawn and he turned and kissed her on both cheeks and they moved away out of sight. Seeing him this way with his family, it was hard to go on fighting and hating him. He was doing what he thought to be right and was prepared to give up his life if it became necessary. He was a man, not the inhuman monster she had been led to believe. It was obvious now that her father had lied, driven by his hatred of the enemy who continually succeeded in escaping capture and by doing so ensured the safety of the King. John's death had not been a cold-blooded murder, but the result of an encounter with a group of Royalists who proved to be the better fighting men. She could not undo the past and she must learn to face the future, bleak as it was, alone, but with her soul washed clean of hatred. She had learned a hard lesson; one she would always remember – as vividly as she would remember the King's Shadow.

"May I come in, Katherine?" Barbara stood in the doorway.

Katherine rose to her feet, her eyes centred on the ball gown the girl was holding.

"Yes, of course."

"I wanted to bring you this. Would you like my maid to dress your hair tonight, or is your girl competent enough?"

"Sarah is quite capable. I am coming to your party because I have to, Barbara, not because I want to. Please don't misunderstand me ... it has nothing to do with you, or your mother ... it's – it's ... "

"Justin," Barbara interrupted smiling. "I know."

"No." Katherine denied the suggestion, her colour heightening. "It is me, and the way I was raised. Look at me. I don't belong in these clothes – in this house ... "

"Because we are Royalists, sworn to protect the King?"

"No, not even that. You could never know what it is like to live with a man like my father. The Bible is the only book he ever reads. He always carries one with him. It rules our lives. There are very few times I can remember my mother laughing ... it was a sin to be happy. She loved to dance, but that was forbidden too and as for wearing pretty clothes – " She broke off, with a bitter laugh. "I watched her grow old before her time. When she could stand my father's harsh ways no longer, she ran away, but he went after her and brought her back. It was the middle of winter. She caught a chill, but he refused to allow a doctor to see her. He said it was God's retribution to make her see the error of her ways. When she died, it was God's will. I loved my mother, Barbara. After her death, alone in the house with him, I could imagine myself becoming like her. John, the man I was to have married, offered me an escape. I was willing to take it. He loved me and I was – fond of him. I would never have been unfaithful and I would have made him happy."

"And when he was killed ... " Barbara nodded understandingly. "No wonder you blamed Justin. I would have too under those circumstances. But what will you do now? Why don't you stay here with us? You have no reason to go back to your father, have you?"

"No. But I couldn't ... he would never allow it."

"After Justin, defying your father should be a simple matter," Barbara answered. "I really am serious. Will you consider it?"

"Your brother would object most strongly – and what about your mother?" It was a mad idea, totally impossible. Why was she even considering it? "No, it would not work."

"The only obstacle is your refusal to accept that it might. Forget it for the moment – come and try on this dress. Justin had it made for me in France last year, but I have lost weight since then and it doesn't fit me. I think it will look very nice on you."

Katherine had to muster every ounce of courage in order to leave her room that evening. At the head of the stairs she faltered and could go no further. She could hear the murmur of voices from the drawing-room and Barbara's infectious laugh, but her trembling legs refused to go on.

"Kate, are you coming down?"

Justin stood below, staring up at her. He was disturbingly handsome in a burgundy velvet coat and breeches. The white lace jabot at his throat seemed to accentuate even more the darkness of his skin. She caught the brilliance of a huge diamond ring on his finger as he put one hand on the banister and came slowly towards her. She had never seen him in such fine attire before. It was a reminder of the contrast between their two worlds, and instinctively she drew back.

"Barbara is asking for you." Halting before her, he held out his hand. Was this a gesture of peace? "You look very beautiful. I thought that dress would be right for you."

She was wearing the dress Barbara had brought, of fine white silk and lace. The bodice and skirt were sewn with hundreds of tiny pearls. It was an excellent fit and accentuated the slender curves of her figure to perfection. The neckline, slashed low across the fullness of her breasts, left bare her smooth arms and shoulders. She was astounded that he had personally chosen it from his sister's wardrobe. Hesitantly she placed her hand in his and allowed him to lead her down to the drawing-room. His touch was firm and oddly reassuring.

"Some old friends of the family have come from St. Cross," he murmured, pausing before the door. "To save everyone embarrassment I have told them you are a friend of mine and sympathetic to our cause. You were hurt while attempting to help the King and I brought you here to recover. In your own interests I suggest you go along with my story."

"Very well." Katherine was inwardly relieved and grateful he had spared her the ordeal of having to face the enmity of his friends.

Upon entering the room he immediately introduced her to the tall woman beside his mother and the young man and girl standing next to them. These guests were Lady Mary de Greville and her daughter Lorette and son Michael, recently returned from Worcester. Katherine's eyes clouded at the sight of the empty sleeve hanging at the latter's side. Yet another casualty of that dreadful day. And then as she stood listening to Justin talking to them, she discovered tragedy had not struck Michael alone. His father had been lost also, and Lorette's husband of one short month. The son had escaped the searching forces of the Lord Protector and successfully returned home where he had been hiding ever since.

As Simon came to claim Katherine's company, she was aware of Justin's intense gaze on her, silently questioning her right to self-pity in the light of what she had learned. Simon gave her little chance to dwell on the disturbing news. For most of the evening he monopolized her. She went into dinner on his arm, sat beside him at the table and afterwards, when they returned to the drawing-room and Elizabeth Douglas played on the spinet, he persuaded her to dance. She did so full of self-consciousness, but he was so gay and friendly that her nervousness soon vanished and she actually began to enjoy herself. Barbara and the King joined her as she stood by the french windows enjoying a breath of cool night air.

"I am glad you were able to join us, Mistress Ashley," Charles said smiling.

"It was at Your Majesty's command."

"That is one privilege of being the King – I can command the company of a beautiful woman whenever I choose. Barbara tells me she has been trying to induce you to stay."

"I have not yet decided." Katherine did not continue, aware that Justin was at her elbow, listening. Charles turned to him with a heavy sigh.

"We will remember this evening, do you not agree, Justin?"

"Indeed, we shall, sire."

"Simon has told me of your wish to remain behind," Charles said and his face was suddenly grave. "I cannot allow it. You will sail with us."

"I will be of more use on this side of the Channel." Justin looked taken aback. Obviously he had not expected his decision to be questioned, even by the King.

"It is my command you accompany us. Now, let us not spoil the evening by further discussion on the subject. This is my dance, I believe, Barbara."

Justin was frowning as he watched his sister move away on the arm of the King, and seemed so angy that Katherine said impulsively:

"If you stay in England you will surely be captured. It can only be a matter of time. It is better you go."

"Have you lost your desire to see my head roll, Kate?" he asked in surprise.

"I was wrong." Katherine's voice was hardly audible. "John's death was not your fault. I no longer feel any hatred for you – everything has gone." Everything! Including the memory of what she had once felt for John himself – all washed away by the kisses of another man. Confused, she turned away from him and went out into the garden. After a moment she heard soft footsteps behind her and knew he was following. She walked to the arbour where she sat down beneath the roses and, looking up, found him standing a few feet away. The fragrance of the flowers was everywhere, carried through the air on a gentle evening breeze. How beautiful it was here! How easy to forget.

"What do you think of my home?" Justin asked. His face was hidden in the shadows, but there was pride in his voice. It was a house to be proud of, as were his family. How she envied him their love and affection.

"It is very lovely."

"Will you stay as Barbara asks?"

So she had told him – or had he known before? Katherine wondered.

"It is impossible."

"Nonsense! If I asked you, would you consider it then, or would I send you running home to the sanctuary of your father's arms?"

"Hardly that."

"So I gather from what I've been told."

Katherine's cheeks burned to think Barbara had related their conversations.

"She had no right to tell you."

"She had every right – she's worried about you." Justin sat beside her – close, but not touching. "Take advantage of the fact you have found a true friend in my sister, Kate, and stay here until you have had a chance to come to terms with what has happened."

"And with myself?"

"From the way you talked to Barbara I think that has

already happened. Will you stay? Or are you anxious to return to the arms of your amorous captain?"

"I would like to stay, but when my father discovers where I am he will come after me," she replied, ignoring the mocking taunt. "He is a vengeful man and might be hard on your mother and sister."

"They are willing to take that chance. Are you?"

Katherine was silent for a long while. Eventually she shook her head.

"No. I have given you my word I will not endanger their lives, and I will keep that pledge. When I leave here I will make up some story that I was shot while escaping from you, and that Sarah cared for me in the forest until I was better. I will say nothing of being here; that way they will not be involved. Sarah will confirm my story if I ask it of her."

"Damnation, but you are a stubborn little witch!"

"Why should you care?" Katherine demanded. "You will be far away."

"And thinking of you every moment of the day. Why do you think I want to stay behind?" Justin demanded in a harsh tone. "I don't want to leave you, but the King has decreed I must, therefore I want to know you are in good hands while I am absent. It might be weeks – months – I pray it will not be years, but if it is, I want to know where you are when I return."

"Don't talk that way," Katherine protested. "There can never be anything between us. You will forget me the moment you leave here."

She tried to stand up, but he caught her by her slender shoulders and held her fast, facing him.

"I shall try, but forgetting you will be impossible."

"I am told French women are not only beautiful, but well skilled in the arts of making men feel wanted." Katherine tried to sound sarcastic and failed miserably.

His soft laughter came out of the darkness only a moment before he bent and took her mouth. She offered no resistance, knowing in her heart that this was what she had wanted all evening. His grip slackened and his arms enfolded her body, pulling her hard against him until she could feel the fierce thudding of his heart. It matched her own. Her hands crept around his neck and her lips answered his – willingly, for the first time.

Before Justin Douglas and Francis, only John had kissed her, but never with such depth of passion – such force as the man who now held her. Her senses reeled. She heard herself cry out, but whether in protest or passion, she did not know. Justin's arms tightened round her until she could scarcely breathe. Soft endearments came between the kisses he pressed on her mouth, her neck, her shoulders and for a while she gave herself without restraint until John's face swam before her, bearing on it an expression so reproachful that she was filled with dread and at once began to struggle to free herself. At the same time a voice cried out inside her – turncoat – sinner – you have allowed yourself to be tempted with sinful pleasures by this man, who killed John Grahaeme. Gentle John, who loved you.

"Justin – no! No!" Katherine almost screamed the words at him and beat her clenched fists against his chest until he released her, his face blank with amazement. Dazed – confused – most of all frightened by her own conflicting emotions, Katherine acted without thinking. Lifting her hand she struck him across both cheeks.

Justin swore savagely and held her away from him. "Have you taken leave of your senses?" he demanded. His eyes narrowed suspiciously, and Katherine's legs grew weak at the fury blazing out of them. "Or is this another act, Kate? Answer me, damn you!"

He shook her so violently that her hair came loose from the combs securing it and tumbled past her ashen face.

"I hate you." She spoke recklessly, tears streaming down over her cheeks, regardless of the consequences. "Do you hear me? I hope they catch you and your beloved King."

She saw disbelief replace anger in Justin's eyes and then, as that faded, the anger returned, more terrifying than before. With a cry she tore herself free and fled towards the house.

CHAPTER SIX

ELIZABETH Douglas spoiled Katherine's hopes that she might be able to slip unnoticed into the house by appearing on the terrace as she came hurrying up the steps.

"There you are. Is Justin with you?"

"Yes – I mean no. He is still out in the garden." Katherine averted her face, conscious of her wet cheeks. "Excuse me, but I have a bad headache. I think I had better go and rest."

"Then I suggest you go through a side door to avoid questions about that very tearful face," Elizabeth said quietly, adding as Katherine turned away: "You won't be able to run away from him for ever, you know."

"He will be gone soon and then I will be free." She did not bother to deny the implication.

"Your heart will never be free. Whether you like it or not it belongs to my son, and if I am any judge of character, I think it always will – no matter what has passed between you."

"It is too late." Katherine lifted her shoulders despondently.

"Because of what has just happened? Nonsense! Have you so little faith in your own emotions?"

"Faith! I have none left," Katherine returned, and her tone was bitter. She was too upset to care that Justin's mother had witnessed the scene beneath the arbour.

"Come with me into the library. We can talk there without being disturbed. You are in no condition to tangle with Justin again and I can see him coming this way."

Taking Katherine's arm, Elizabeth Douglas led her quickly around the side of the house and into the library. Closing the windows, she turned to look at the young girl perched tentatively on the arm of a chair.

"I did not mean to witness what seemed to be a very private

moment, but the sight of my son holding you in his arms has both surprised and pleased me and aroused memories of my own tempestuous courtship. Justin is like his father and will never allow a woman to rule him, which is one of the reasons I know he has never become seriously involved with anyone before. He values his freedom, yet now he seems willing to abandon it. Why did you slap him?" Elizabeth sat down, carefully arranging the skirts of her saffron gown about her. "You don't have to tell me, of course, but you may find it helps to talk."

"I had – to make him – let me go." Katherine felt her cheeks burn scarlet as she spoke. Her lips still felt bruised from Justin's kisses.

"Are you so afraid of him?"

"It isn't a question of fear. Not any more."

"What then?"

"I don't seem able to grasp what has happened to me. One minute I am so sure of my feelings, but as soon as I think of my father, or John, the man I was to have married, it all seems so wrong. My being here with you, I mean. I don't belong here and I have no right to care for Justin. Suppose I remained in this house after his departure and he was caught, perhaps by my father. It would affect our relationship, would it not? And if Justin was hurt – or my father? Can either of us say how we would react?"

"Justin is a soldier. He is not afraid of death. As for me, I have already lost a husband and I pray to God nothing will happen to either of my sons, but if it does they will be victims of the war like so many others and I will not attribute blame to any one particular person."

"How can you talk of losing them so – so calmly?" Katherine asked, aghast.

"Would it help them – or me – to be more emotional? You have come to a cross-road in your life, Katherine. It happens to us all, sometimes more than once. Along one road you could walk with Justin, but you do not know where it will lead you or what dangers lie hidden round each bend. You must decide if you have the necessary courage to take the first step. To love him is not enough. Like his father Justin will expect – no, demand – you give yourself completely. I think you are everything he has ever sought in a woman and that is why he has so far refused to acknowledge how he feels, knowing that once he does he will be totally committed."

"Is – is that how it was for you?" Katherine asked quietly, and saw Elizabeth's eyes soften.

"I would have done anything my husband asked of me – gone anywhere with him. It was an understanding between us. In actual fact he asked very little of me, but he knew and the knowledge gave our marriage something special. I was married when I was seventeen, and Justin was born a year later. My husband gave me this house on his first birthday. All our children were born here. The old place is full of many wonderful memories."

Katherine stood up, her hands locked tightly together in front of her. She had memories too, but they were difficult to erase from her mind.

"I want more than mere memories."

"Then you have the alternative road – the one you know, the safe one." Elizabeth got up and crossed to her side. Gently she put her hands over Katherine's and looked into her pale face. "You and Justin have faced danger together – even death. Can you honestly tell me you can turn your back on him and walk away – back to your father whom you fear and a way of life you detest?"

"No – no." Katherine whispered brokenly. "Help me, please. What must I do? I hurt him tonight, deliberately. I was afraid – unsure. How do I know he will forgive me?"

"You don't know. You must make your decision and stand by it. That way he will know you are sincere. He will trust you and accept that what you say is the truth. Are you in love with him?"

"Yes."

"No doubts?"

"Not now. You were right, it has helped to talk about it. You must think me very foolish."

"My dear child, when one is in love, it is permissible to be contrary."

Katherine looked towards the window, wondering if Justin had returned to the drawing-room yet. The memory of the fury blazing out of his dark eyes undermined her new-found courage.

"I don't think I can face him yet."

"The longer you wait, the worse it will be. Justin is a formidable opponent, but you must set things right between you before he leaves. Go upstairs and freshen your face first. Wait – before you go, there is something I think you should have."

Mystified, Katherine watched her cross the room to a small rosewood chest of three drawers standing against the far wall. Unlocking the top one, Elizabeth pushed her hand to the back and drew something out. Katherine's eyes widened as she came back and held out a gold locket and chain. It was identical to the one Justin wore.

"I see you recognize it. My husband had them made for our first wedding anniversary." Elizabeth opened it with loving care and both women looked down at the miniatures nestled there. One was of Justin – the other of an older man with greying hair. They were so alike that Katherine knew it had to be his father. "Two identical lockets. We always wore them. It was his way of keeping us together, even when we were separated. He was part of me. I had only to touch this to be near him – that's how it was for him too. It was his wish Justin should take his when he died. To my knowledge he has worn it since that day. I think it only right you should have mine."

"I can't," Katherine protested. "It is so precious to you."

"I have my memories. One day, when you have yours, you can pass this on to your child." Ignoring her protest, Elizabeth fastened the clasp around Katherine's neck. "Wear it and be one with Justin as I was with my husband."

"Won't he – Justin – be angry?"

"When he sees you have it, he will know you both have my blessing. I think that will count for something."

Impulsively Katherine leaned forward and lightly brushed the other woman's cheeks with her lips.

"Thank you for making things so easy for me."

"You may not thank me years from now when you have a

difficult husband on your hands," Elizabeth answered with a soft laugh.

As they came out of the library, Barbara was just crossing the hall.

"Mother, where is Justin? He hasn't danced with me yet."

"I thought he was with you."

"He came back for a little while, then disappeared again."

"He was in the garden with me," Katherine explained. She felt dismayed that he was still so angry he should have chosen solitude instead of the gay atmosphere of the drawing-room. What chance would she have with him in such a mood?

"Why don't you go and find him?" Elizabeth asked meaningly.

"Where should I look?"

"There's a place Justin always goes to when he wants to be alone. Go out through the west door of the garden and follow the path through the trees. Beyond is a lake and a small hunting lodge. I'm sure he will be there."

"Shall I show you? Justin and I used to play there as children," Barbara offered. Her offer was met with a fierce frown from her mother and she looked puzzled, but then as her eyes fell on the object suspended around Katherine's neck, she understood.

"I think I will go upstairs first," Katherine said. "Will you make my excuses to the others, please, Lady Douglas?

"Of course, my dear." Elizabeth turned away smiling and took Barbara's hand. "The King will think we have deserted him."

Alone in her bedroom Katherine sat down by the window and waited for the wild beating of her heart to subside. She was unsure what Justin's reaction would be when she sought him out, but she knew it had to be done. She loved him! The King's Shadow – the most wanted man in the country, next to the King. It would not be easy to live in his mother's house knowing the danger he must face in order to get his sovereign to France, but she had shared it too and that bond linked them together. She understood the fierce passion which urged him on to risk his life for Charles – even now it burned in her breast. To save Justin she would risk anything – even her own life, because without him she was nothing. This was not how it had been with John. This time she belonged. Without Justin she was not a whole person. It was strange to sit in the darkness and dissect her emotions, but necessary, because once she was with Justin, it would be impossible to remain composed. He had only to look at her as he had in the garden, to set her heart racing again. And against his kisses she had no defence – she no longer needed any. She wanted him to hold her and convince her this was reality and not a fanciful dream.

Unnoticed, she slipped out of the house and hurried along the path to the door set in the garden wall. It swung back on well-oiled hinges, and she passed through. Ahead was a narrow, well-trodden path leading into the trees, exactly as Elizabeth described it. Picking up her skirts, Katherine carefully set off along it. After twenty yards, the trees thinned out and she found herself standing at the edge of a lake. The waters shimmered in the moonlight and she stood for a long moment enjoying the tranquillity of the place. The lodge was to her right and she glimpsed a faint light shining from one of the windows. As she moved towards it she had visions of the Douglases here on a summer's day; Justin and his mother walking beside the lake, Simon lazing by the lodge, Barbara picking flowers. Perhaps one day she would share these things with them – she hoped so.

The well-worn door swung open at her touch and she stepped inside. In front of her a solitary candle burned on a table, beside a bottle of wine and a large silver goblet, with the contents untouched. There was no sign of Justin. As she turned, the door slammed behind her and he stepped out of the shadows, sheathing the knife which seconds before had been aimed at her back.

"I wasn't expecting company." He stared into her shocked face for a moment before moving past her to pick up his drink. "How did you know where to find me?"

"Your mother told me."

"Did she? So she's playing matchmaker again, is she?"

Justin swallowed the dry burgundy and refilled the goblet. He did not look at her. He looked angry with her for intruding on his private domain.

"That isn't fair," Katherine protested. "She is a wonderful person. I have grown very fond of her in the short time I have been here."

"But she is mistaken in her belief that I harbour some deep feelings for you," Justin replied cruelly.

Katherine moved closer to him. She was quite calm and in control of herself. Having come this far she did not intend to turn and run, even though his attitude made her want to.

"She saw us together in the garden."

"No wonder she's making marriage plans." He wheeled on her suddenly, his mouth twisted into a bitter line. "What do you want?"

"To talk – to explain."

He ran his fingers over the cheeks where she had struck him.

"You said everything very clearly." His eyes narrowed sharply as he saw his mother's locket and its full implication struck him. Katherine had hoped it would make things easier between them, but if anything they became worse. Leaning back against the table, his arms folded across his chest, he demanded ungraciously: "Well – what have you to say?"

"Why are you still so angry? You said once you didn't want us to fight."

"Perhaps I'm seeing you clearly for the first time. It's surprising how a good hearty slap can clear the mists from a fool's eyes."

"You are not a fool, but you are proud – too proud to admit what your mother said is true, and that if I had not lost my head and slapped you we might have been more honest with each other."

"Honest!" Justin drawled mockingly. "When did you acquire that virtue?"

Katherine flushed, but went on determinedly. "I've come to terms with myself at last. John was no more than an escape from my father. There – is that what you want to hear?"

"And having relieved your conscience by admitting it, you

can tuck him away in some corner of your tidy little mind and forget him. I vow you won't forget me so easily," Justin said, straightening, and at the glitter which sprang to his eyes she instinctively stepped back. What devil possessed him now? "No, don't move away, Kate. You came here for a specific purpose and I want to know what it is."

"I came to talk – to apologize for behaving so childishly," Katherine answered lamely.

His tall frame dwarfed her, robbing her of words she so desperately wanted to say. He came closer and, reaching out, caught both her wrists in one strong hand and held her fast.

"Shall I tell you why you are here? To make sure you didn't jeopardize your own precious skin. Well, you haven't. I'm not a vindictive man and I'll keep my word."

"I didn't come for that."

"Liar!" He shook her roughly, then swept her hard against him and pressed his mouth against her cheek, her hair, the smooth hollow of her throat. "Damn you! Damn you!"

"Justin – please! Let me go!" Katherine tried to free her hands. She wanted to put them about his neck, confess her love and end this farce between them, but as his grip tightened she realized he had mistaken the action.

"What's wrong, Kate? There's no one watching us this time," he taunted.

"Oh, you fool! Listen to me ... " Katherine was near to tears.

He kissed her into silence and she immediately became still, her lips flaring to life beneath his. He muttered a savage oath and drew back. In the candlelight his features were suddenly pale.

"Why don't you slap me again, Kate?"

"I don't want to. I love you, Justin."

"Don't talk to me of love." He caught her face in his hands and kissed her again. This time there was no passion in his kisses – no tenderness. It was a deliberate attempt to show her the contempt he felt for her, and he succeeded. Releasing her, he pushed her roughly towards the door. "Get out before I treat you as you deserve."

Katherine stumbled blindly against a chair on her way out and was blinded by tears as she reeled unsteadily out of the door. Picking up her skirts she ran from the lodge and into the sanctuary of the trees, not stopping until forced to do so by lack of breath, and then she sank down onto the ground and wept bitterly.

The subsidence of tears left her weak and ashamed and she sat with her back against a tree trunk until her eyes were dry and she had stopped trembling. How long she stayed there she did not know. It might have been ten or fifteen minutes, but was probably more like an hour, she realized, as she climbed to her feet to go back to the house. She could not find the path, but in her present state of mind she did not care, and continued to wander aimlessly through the trees, oblivious to the hem of her beautiful gown being caught on thorny bramble bushes. He had sent her away – scorned her. He was not only blind, but made of stone too or he would have seen she spoke the truth – felt it when he held her and her lips answered his. He did not want to believe her. Perhaps his change of attitude had been a deliberate move in order to protect his mother and sister. He had her promise now that she would not involve them and, no matter what he thought of her, she would not break her word. Perhaps one day another woman would stand before him as she had earlier, with the same lovelight in her eyes, and he would see it and know how wrong he had been.

Katherine came out of the protection of the trees and found herself on the hill overlooking the house. The lights shone clearly below, but it was at least half a mile away – she had been walking in the wrong direction! She was about to move on when a sound suspiciously like a groan came from some bushes to the right of her. Cautiously she approached and peered over the top. A man lay at her feet, his face covered in blood where he had been brutally beaten over the head.

"Who are you?" She bent and touched his shoulder. Instinctively she knew he was dying. "Who did this to you?"

"Soldiers ... warn the house. Soldiers ... " His voice trailed off and Katherine knew he would never speak again.

She straightened, wiping her hand across her skirt to erase the streak of blood there.

Soldiers! Then this man must have been the look-out posted by Justin to keep watch. Her eyes searched the darkness below the hill. She could see nothing, hear no movement, but they were there somewhere, waiting for the right moment to attack. The King would be captured; Justin too. They would have no warning, no chance to use their secret way of escape. She wheeled and ran back the way she had come, praying Justin was still at the lodge. Hampered by her skirts, she stumbled and fell, got up and ran on, rubbing a bruised shoulder. Her heart was pounding by the time she reached the lake. The lodge was in darkness. She stood in the doorway and called his name, but there was no answer, and she fought down the panic rising inside her.

A single shot echoed through the still night air, followed by a volley of gunfire – then another. By the time Katherine reached the garden door her legs were ready to collapse beneath her. She leaned against it, gasping for breath. Her chest hurt and her throat was so dry that she had no voice to scream a warning to the inhabitants of the house. A sheet of flame leapt from one of the windows, rousing her from her brief rest.

"Justin – Barbara, Simon, where are you?" She began to shout as she staggered along the path. A soldier came from the direction of the lawn and blocked her way. She struggled against the hand which grasped her arm and began dragging her round to the other side of the house. "Let me go!"

"Stop struggling, or I'll knock you cold," the trooper growled. "It's too late to warn your friends."

Too late! Katherine's senses reeled under the shock of his words. Bending her head, she sank her teeth into the back of his hand. As he released her with an oath, she pushed him violently backwards and he tripped and fell.

"Katherine! Here, child." A hand grasped Katherine's skirts, pulling her backwards into the bushes. "Follow me, quickly!"

Elizabeth Douglas's face was streaked with smoke and dirt,

her beautiful yellow gown torn, her hair in disarray. Katherine stumbled after her, biting her lips to hold back a cry of pain as a low branch caught her across the head, striking the still tender scar on her temple.

"Wait! Oh, please wait! Where is Justin?"

"Safe with Simon and the King."

"Then you must save yourself and Barbara. Don't worry about me – they won't harm me when I tell them who I am."

A musket shot whistled through the trees above her head, drowning her words. Two troopers appeared on the path in front of them.

"Run!" Katherine begged. "For the love of God ... run ..."

She tripped and fell to the ground, nursing a bruised ankle as Justin's mother turned and ran through the bushes. Another man broke through the trees, levelling a pistol at her back. Katherine's scream mingled with the sound of the shot, and before her horrified eyes Elizabeth Douglas collapsed in a motionless heap.

"You have killed her!" Huge tears trembled in her eyes as she stared up into the cold features of Captain Francis Grahaeme. "Are you proud of yourself ... you murderer?"

"Hold your tongue, mistress, or I'll have you bound and gagged until you are calmer and in a more receptive mood for my questions."

Katherine shook her head, dazedly trying to gather her reeling senses.

"Let me go to her." She was pushed back as she moved towards the inert figure of the woman who had shown her such kindness. Francis Grahaeme barked out an order and she was hauled to her feet by one of his men and forcibly propelled along the path. She was too weak to offer further resistance. A terrible sight met her eyes as they came to the front of the house. Hungry flames were leaping skywards from the windows and the roof; the whole lower floors were a sheet of white fire. She realized it would not take long for the whole building to be devastated. She could still hear shooting, and there were soldiers everywhere poking the bushes with their muskets and swords.

"Katherine." She turned her head as someone called her name, and saw that Barbara was also a captive.

The officer at her side spun around to watch the arrival of the new prisoner, and Katherine's heart grew cold with fear as recognition dawned on her. The hard face which regarded her bore no trace of compassion for her dishevelled state or the callous way she was manhandled by the soldier who held her. She knew from past experience this man was beyond pity. Only he could stand by and watch a fine old house consumed with fire and do nothing to prevent it. He was capable of the most inhuman acts in the name of God. In His name he had killed his own wife.

"Where did you find this one?"

"In the garden, Major. She was yelling at someone in the house. She must have slipped out earlier."

"Did you not hear any names, man?"

"Yes, sir. Simon was one and I think Justin . . . yes, that's right. Justin and Simon."

"Leave her with me and join the others. I want those men found – they can't have gone far."

"You haven't caught them!" Katherine breathed, and smiled bravely at Barbara. "Did you hear? They are still free."

The other girl nodded. She had a large bruise on one cheek and she was as dishevelled as Katherine. She too had fought against the soldiers who burst into the house and seized her, and it had taken three of them to carry her kicking and screaming out into the garden. In the hectic struggle a candle-lamp had been dashed to the floor, but the fire had not been discovered until more soldiers tried to enter the house and found the doorway a mass of flames.

"So – you are not a prisoner after all?" Nathaniel Ashley stared bleakly into his daughter's defiant features. "Your friends led us quite a chase. The reports I received led me to believe you were a prisoner of Justin Douglas – that was until one of my patrols encountered your coachman Peter. He told quite a different story – a story I refused to believe . . . but I see now he was telling the truth. You were not leading them into a trap, were you, but doing your best to aid Royalist fugitives – the most wanted men in England – to reach a place of safety."

Katherine glanced down at her ruined ball gown. It was torn and streaked with blood, and she had lost a shoe in her headlong flight from the lake. She felt exhausted, but knew she must find fresh courage from somewhere to fight the formidable foe who now threatened her. He was no longer her father, but her enemy – Justin's enemy. There was nothing he could do to her except perhaps beat her for disgracing him before his troops, and even that was a small thing. So long as Justin remained free, she would be willing to face any penalty. Barbara's safety was important too. She looked frightened and lost. There was the possibility of her being sent to London and imprisoned. Katherine made up her mind that would not happen. How she would prevent it she did not know, but she would.

"Your reports were not misleading, father – I was his prisoner." Katherine chose her words carefully. Under the circumstances it was useless to try and deny she had been used to manoeuvre the escape of the King; but she was determined to extricate Barbara and her mother as much as possible from the damning situation.

"Then what are you doing here – dressed like a court whore?"

A wave of scarlet colour flooded into Katherine's cheeks, and she heard Barbara gasp in horror.

"I was hurt – shot by a trooper somewhere near here, while trying to escape. I was brought here unconscious and Lady Douglas cared for me. You cannot blame me for my presence here – I was given no alternative. As for the clothes – I can hardly go around with nothing on, can I?"

"Silence! How dare you speak to me in such a fashion?" Nathaniel Ashley snapped harshly. Katherine knew he had not expected defiance – not open defiance anyway. Since the death of her mother he had grown accustomed to her silent insolence, but this was something totally new. She realized he had not recognized her at first, and the fact that he had mistaken her for a Royalist woman made him furious. She had her mother's bearing and elegance, the kind of breeding no simple woman should possess. Over the years he had tried unsuccessfully to beat all femininity out of her. She saw his lips tighten as he stared at the torn neckline of her gown, which gaped over the fullness of one breast. "Find something to put around your shoulders! You are making a disgusting exhibition of yourself!"

A soldier emerged from the undergrowth and called to him: "We have someone here, sir!"

Motioning a dragoon to stand guard over the two prisoners, he hurried across the lawn. Katherine took Barbara in her arms and hugged her reassuringly.

"It's going to be all right," she whispered. "Be brave." She baulked at telling Barbara her mother had been killed.

"Is – is he really your father?" Barbara stared after the Puritan Major, her expression shocked.

"Yes."

"He looks at you as if he – he hates you."

"I think he does. You must not concern yourself with me – I won't be harmed. Tell me what happened. I left Justin in the lodge and went for a walk. I found the look-out dead and came back to warn Justin, but he had already come back to the house."

"Mother came to warn you. Didn't you see her? Oh, Katherine, I'm frightened. It all happened so quickly. Did you say our man on the hill is dead? They must have killed him and then surrounded the house. Simon saw someone in the garden – that gave us a few minutes' grace. He and the King went into the tunnel. I had scarcely closed the entrance after Justin when the soldiers burst in and dragged me outside."

Katherine felt tears rise to her eyes in relief. Justin was safe!

"There's Sarah!" she cried, and a moment later the maid was running towards them through the smoke, to collapse sobbing on her mistress's shoulder.

"Mistress Katherine, I thought you had been shot."

"Hush, Sarah! As you can see, I am unhurt. Have you heard anything about the others? We think they have escaped."

"No. I ran out after Lady Douglas to try and find you, and then I heard shots. I think she was hit, but I'm not sure, and then the soldiers grabbed me. Captain Grahaeme is with them. He gave orders to shoot anyone who tried to run away."

Barbara uttered a distressed cry and pressed her hands against her mouth.

"Mother!"

"She was shot, Barbara. I'm sorry . . . " There was no easy way to deliver the dreadful news. "She was on her way to join Justin when – " Katherine broke off, overcome with emotion.

"Katherine, come here," Nathaniel Ashley ordered, from a few yards away.

"Stay with Barbara," Katherine whispered to her maid, and went to join him.

He moved back as she approached, allowing her to see the motionless figure which lay face down on the ground. Katherine swayed, fighting down the nausea which swept over her at the wanton murder of the woman who had so readily befriended her, and the shame because she bore the same name as the man who led the attack on the house. Justin's mother dead – his home collapsing in flames behind her – his sister a prisoner! Her fingers closed round the locket at her throat and she closed her eyes and prayed.

A stinging blow across the cheek snapped back her head and she stared up at her father, her lovely face contorted with pain and grief.

"Identify her."

"Lady Douglas. Murdered by Francis Grahaeme."

"She was shot attempting to escape. There will be others before this night is over." Captain Grahaeme came out of the trees, pistol in hand. He gave her no more than a cursory glance.

"She came to help me," Katherine whispered. "Only a coward would use a pistol on a woman's back."

Her father hardly heard her, she realized. His eyes flickered past her to the open garden door and the path leading into the trees.

"You were coming from that direction. Who were you out

there with? Why are you so important that she risked her life to come and find you? By Heaven, girl, if you don't answer me, I'll beat it out of you."

"Why not, it wouldn't be the first time you have taken a stick to me, would it, Father? If you must know I was with Justin Douglas. Don't waste time looking for him – he is long gone. When he found the man you had killed, he knew you were here. I came back alone to warn the others while he escaped."

"You lie!" her father interrupted harshly. "You came running back calling out his name. You thought he was here. Admit it – you tried to warn him!"

"Yes – and I'd do it again. It makes me sick to look at all this – to know my father leads men who kill and burn like mad animals. These people took me in and cared for me. They were kind, but you wouldn't understand what that means. To you kindness is a weakness, to be shut out of your life and beaten out of mine. You have failed, Father."

"Go on. With each word you betray yourself further."

"I don't care. Don't you realize that?" Katherine cried. "You used your own hatred to turn me into something horrible, seeking revenge for John's death. I believe it was the only way you could tie me to you – a bond of hatred – the same desire for revenge. You almost destroyed me; but for Justin you might have succeeded."

"So you are involved with this man. You know who he is, don't you?"

"The King's Shadow. Yes, I know." Katherine was oblivious to the troopers listening around her – uncaring that her admitted link with Justin exposed her as a turncoat – a traitor. "In the beginning I set out to trap him, not for you, for myself. I wanted to watch him die for John's murder, but it wasn't the way you told me, was it? A man like Justin Douglas does not kill in cold blood. Now I know the truth I am ashamed at what I tried to do – and if I can make up for it in some way, I will."

It was done – she was committed, and looking at the faces all around her, she saw she was condemned.

CHAPTER SEVEN

THE house of Major Nathaniel Ashley was situated on the outskirts of Newbury. It had once belonged to a wealthy merchant, loyal to Charles I, whose home and business had been confiscated by Cromwell to help settle the enormous sum of back pay owing to his troops. The house and the considerable acreage of ground surrounding it had been a reward to the Major for services rendered.

It was a pleasant-looking house and the rooms were large and airy, but Katherine had never liked it. She occupied the top floor which consisted of five rooms, of which only two were in use. On the floor below were her father's rooms, the library and the sitting-room and the spacious dining-room where she often entertained his army colleagues. The ground floor contained his study and the servants' quarters, with the kitchen alongside. A housekeeper, two kitchen maids and Katherine's own maid, Sarah, were the only servants.

With her father often working into the early hours of the morning, there were times when Katherine did not see him for days – weeks, when he led his men off to fight and she sat alone in her rooms wondering if she would ever see him again.

It had taken many months of painstaking labour to turn her two rooms into a complete world, set apart from the floors below. Once the door of her bedroom closed behind her, she was surrounded by things chosen with great care to make her self-imposed exile more pleasant – and she felt secure. At least that was how it had been before her involvement with Justin Douglas and his family. Now, with his mother dead, his sister a prisoner in a room along the corridor, and with no way of knowing if the man she loved was alive or dead, Katherine felt desperately vulnerable and helpless.

Surrounded by her father's men, in a carriage commandeered from the nearby village, Katherine, Barbara and Sarah had been driven away from the Douglas house, where smoke still spiralled skywards from the blackened ruins and the unmarked grave where Elizabeth Douglas had been hurriedly buried. The journey was a nightmare for Katherine, who feared news of their capture might have been leaked deliberately to the local population in the hope that Justin and Simon would come to the aid of their sister, but they reached Newbury without incident.

Despite Barbara's collapse at her mother's graveside and the fever which developed on the journey, she was confined in one of the rooms near Katherine and denied the comforting presence of her friends. Katherine's entreaties to be allowed to remain with her were ignored by her father and resulted in her being locked in her rooms for two days and deprived of the services of her maid. During that time she was brought only one meal, of plain, unappetizing food and water to drink. She had endured such treatment before for disobedient behaviour, and she bore it without protest, but during the long hours as she sat trying to occupy her mind with a book or needlework, she gradually grew more indignant at the cruelty being shown to the unfortunate girl who had fallen into her father's hands.

On the third day Sarah was allowed to return to her. She brought news of the doctor who had been summoned to attend Barbara and of the soldiers who now guarded the house. Three in all, two on the ground floor and another at the rear entrance. Katherine was in no doubt her father would send Barbara to London the moment she was well enough. Before that could happen Katherine knew she had somehow to effect an escape for the girl. There would be Royalist sympathizers in the town, but she did not know how to contact them and she doubted very much if she would be allowed to leave the house.

The following evening she waited for the doctor to arrive, and then slipped into Barbara's room on his heels.

"Dr Richardson?" She moved to the foot of the bed, lifting her gaze from Barbara's sleeping form to the man who stood at the side, his hand on her wrist. He was a short, plump man in his middle fifties with a pair of brown eyes that rested on her curiously. She had often seen him before and knew his wife as a passing acquaintance. Where his loyalties lay she did not know, but the risk in finding out was minimal – she had already proclaimed her change of heart.

"Yes."

"I am Katherine Ashley. How – how is my friend today?"

"A little better. She should be able to get up in a day or two."

"Oh no! I mean – are you sure? She was so ill on the journey here. Shouldn't she rest in bed for at least a week?"

The doctor closed his bag and turned away from the bed. His lack of concern irritated her.

"The Major wishes her to be ready to travel before then. The shock of her mother's death will soon pass."

"No, it will not," Katherine said in a low, angry voice. "Not for her – or for me. We will not find it easy to forget the senseless destruction of homes and people."

"Hardly the sentiments I would expect from the daughter of Nathaniel Ashley," Dr Richardson returned with a frown. "The girl comes from an infamous family – why, one of her brothers is the notorious rogue known as the King's Shadow, is he not?"

"You are well informed, doctor."

"It did not take long for news of what happened to get around."

"And you condone it?"

"I am a doctor, Mistress Ashley, not a soldier. Whenever possible I save lives and stay out of politics. For the moment this girl is my patient. When she is well she will be your father's responsibility once more. What happens to her is none of my concern."

"And so, like Pontius Pilate, you wash your hands of her," Katherine said bitterly.

"Are you so innocent you can sit in judgment on me? The whole town knows how you tried to trap Sir Justin and the King."

"That isn't possible . . . " Katherine's voice trailed off into silence as an awful thought leapt into her mind. For three days she had had no communication with the outside world, and Sarah also had been refused permission to leave the house. They had both been deliberately confined so that her father could salvage his pride. It was the only answer. He was feared by his men, and that fear would keep secret what had happened at the Douglas house. Her defiant outburst had achieved nothing. She was as much a prisoner as Barbara, with about as much hope for leniency. Wordlessly she turned away, biting her lips to keep back the tears.

"You may tell the Major that Mistress Douglas will be ready to travel in two days," Dr Richardson said, moving towards the door. "Good day, Mistress Ashley."

Katherine wanted to scream as the door closed behind him. His words had left her in no doubt that he thought she had been testing his loyalty on the instructions of her father. What kind of a world did they live in when people were so afraid to help each other? she thought miserably.

"Katherine – don't go."

Barbara was awake, stretching out her hand appealingly, and Katherine went to reassure her. She had never felt so helpless as she did at that moment. The poor girl was terrified – not without good reason.

"I heard you talking. It was kind of you to try and help me, but I know it is hopeless." Barbara managed a faint smile. She was still very pale, and the hand which smoothed back her hair trembled visibly. "You must not alienate yourself from your father any more. When I have gone, you still have to live here with him."

"He doesn't matter. Did you hear the doctor? My father has already begun to protect himself from my actions. Before long everyone will believe I was part of his plan to capture the King – that it was my intention to lead them into his trap."

"We know that isn't true."

"But Justin doesn't," Katherine said. "He has never really trusted me, and when he hears these rumours he will hate and despise me."

"Justin cares for you." Barbara sat up in bed, clearly puzzled.

So much had happened that she had not had a chance to ask Katherine what had taken place when she had met Justin in the lodge.

"No, you are wrong. I told him I loved him, but he didn't believe me. Why should he after the way I acted? I do love him, Barbara, but I have no way of proving it to him now. I pray to God he will get safely to France. So long as he is alive, what he thinks of me is unimportant."

"You must not deny this story your father has put about," Barbara said. "It is his way of protecting you too."

"He is only thinking of himself. Why should I allow everyone to believe such a monstrous lie?"

"To deny it would make you an outcast among people you have probably known all your life. It is different for me – I am prepared to accept the consequences. I am to be taken to London then?"

"Somehow I will prevent that happening." Katherine rose to her feet, a determined look on her face. "Try to rest, you will need all your strength."

As Katherine entered her sitting-room, Nathaniel Ashley turned from the window to look at her. She halted just inside the door, her eyes widening at the scene which met her eyes. The room had been stripped of all the little luxuries she had installed. The curtains and the pretty matching cushions she had made were gone. Every single one of her books had been removed as well as her needlework table and the sampler she had been working on that day. The floor was devoid of carpet, and all but essential furniture had been removed. A couch, the table and two chairs were all that remained. Her father did not speak. She knew the look of horror on her face gave him great satisfaction. She stumbled into the bedroom and found it had undergone similar treatment. The beautiful drapes which had adorned the bed and dressing-table had been torn away. The closet door was open and all but four of her dresses removed. She noticed that the ones which remained were the plainest she possessed.

"You set too much store on worldly goods, Katherine. You are like your mother." She turned and stared coldly at her father. He had struck her where it hurt most, reminding her how inhuman he was towards those who opposed his will. She stared at the long blackthorn stick he carried in one hand, and then at the open Bible on the table beside him. It meant she was to be chastised for her sins. "Go down on your knees, Katherine, and beg God's forgiveness."

When she did not move, Nathaniel Ashley grasped her by the arm and forced her to the floor. Katherine bore the blows in silence, shutting her mind against the pain which seared her body. Her spirit was uncrushable, her resolution to save Barbara unshaken by the methodical beating which left her lying sick and faint across her bed.

It was growing dark when she opened her eyes. Someone had lighted an oil lamp on the table and drawn the curtains. As she sat up she became aware of a figure reclining in a chair in the halflight in front of the window.

"Was it worth it, Katherine?" Francis Grahaeme's voice mocked her from the shadows. "What price your King's man now?"

"What do you want?" Katherine barely suppressed a cry as she tried to raise a hand to brush back the hair from her face. She was so stiff she could scarcely climb off the bed, and every movement was like having a thousand sharp needles pushed into her skin. She had forgotten he was now residing beneath her father's roof.

"Your father is a fool. I told him a beating would do no good."

"Why do you care what he does to me?"

"Always you try to make me out a heartless ogre," Francis returned amusedly. Rising to his feet, he turned up the oil lamp and stood looking into her pale face. "I could help – if you wish it."

"I imagine the price you ask will be too high," Katherine retorted and saw a flash of annoyance on the weatherbeaten features. He was older than John by five years. For ten years the army had been his life. Slowly his ambition to reach the top of his chosen profession was coming true. The campaign in Ireland had brought promotion to captain, and before Worcester she had heard a rumour of his being appointed to Cromwell's personal staff. That meant London. She knew Francis liked the city life where his appetite for women and gambling could be satisfied without any gossip.

"I shall ask no more from you than you were prepared to give my brother."

Katherine stared at him in amazement. Was he asking her to marry him?

"Why not?" A sardonic smile touched Francis's wide mouth. "Perhaps you have not heard, but I am being considered for the staff of the Lord Protector himself. He thinks highly of me. I could go far, Katherine."

"But you need a wife to give you the cloak of respectability. Oliver Cromwell prefers family men about him. God-fearing, church-going men. Is that to be your new image, Francis?"

"It could mean a new life for you, away from this mausoleum. All you have to do is substitute me for John."

"And go from one prison to another."

Francis Grahaeme's eyes swept her from head to toe, and his look made her inwardly shudder.

"It need not be that way. You know I have always wanted you . . ."

"I don't love you."

"You didn't love John, but you were about to marry him." He had caught her in his arms before she could step back and drawn her against his chest. "Are you thinking of your Royalist lover? Close your eyes, pretend it is him kissing you, if it helps, though I'll warrant you'll not remember the taste of his embraces for long."

His kisses failed to arouse any response to her stiff lips, but she was too weak and bruised to struggle, and endured his embrace in silent misery.

"You cold bitch!" He pushed her away from him, such fury on his face that she thought he might strike her. "Be damned then – I won't lift a finger to help you."

"Go away, Francis. Go away and leave me in peace. Find

some other poor unsuspecting woman to wed you, for I never will."

Dr Richardson did not call at the house the next day, but the morning after, as he left Barbara's room, Sarah waylaid him and showed him into the sitting-room. Katherine allowed him a long moment to stare around the bare room before gesturing to the maid to leave them alone.

"How is the Lady Barbara this morning, doctor?"

"I shall be informing the Major she is well enough to travel."

"From one prison to another." She had used those words about herself. How alike their lives were becoming.

The doctor's eyes narrowed sharply as he stared at the sombrely dressed figure before him.

"What is it you want of me, Mistress Ashley?"

"Time. I need time. Three or four days at least – longer if possible."

"Which it is not. The Major is not a fool – nor am I. This is another of his devious schemes to weed out Royalist sympathizers, is it not? He has used you once, why not again?"

Katherine motioned to the room around them.

"Is this the way a father rewards a dutiful daughter, Dr Richardson? I have been deprived of everything except the barest necessities, as you can see. The story my father has allowed to circulate is only partly true. It was my intention to trap the King and his friends, and I would have succeeded but for the cleverness of the man you call the King's Shadow. How glad I am I did not succeed, for I have come to realize the narrowness and selfishness of the world in which my father and I have lived for so long. The night my father sprang his trap at the Douglas house, I tried to warn them, but it was too late."

"He says you arranged for the whole family and the King to be gathered beneath one roof – that you had gained their trust."

"Men like Justin Douglas do not trust easily, doctor. In effect I was his prisoner. I was with him only a short while before the troopers attacked the house. If I had planned it with my father, would I have left the house with the man whose capture is as important to him as that of the King?"

"Why do you tell me all this? It means nothing to me."

"If you are loyal to my father then you will tell him of this conversation. Perhaps he will send me away too. It would be best that way. If you are not . . . if as I hope and pray you do not have the heart to send that poor girl to London, then you will give me the time I need."

"To do what? Effect an escape for her? How will you do that with armed guards around the house?"

"I will think of something. Will you tell my father she is not yet ready to travel?" Katherine pleaded. If he was against her she was lost, and for a brief moment she had visions of accompanying Barbara to prison.

The man did not answer. Turning on his heel he opened the door – and her heart sank. Outside Sarah stood on watch. Seeing her, he stepped back and closed the door again.

"I can give you five days, no more. I will leave some medicine for you which will induce a temperature – only slight, but sufficient to keep her confined to bed. The rest is up to you."

"Bless you!" Katherine breathed. "I shall never forget your kindness. I have nothing to give you except my thanks. My father has taken everything of value from me – wait!" From inside the high-collared dress she wore Katherine drew out the locket Elizabeth Douglas had given her, and unfastened it. She had worn it continually since that day. "This was given to me by a very wonderful woman. Take it, please – it is the only thing of value I possess."

Dr Richardson took it from her and stared down at the engraved crest on one side. Slowly turning it over in his open palm he opened it and looked down at the two miniatures. The eyes which glanced up at Katherine were no longer suspicious.

"The crest is known to me. I believe what you have told me, and I will help you all I can. Take this back – I can see by your face it means a great deal to you."

"You – you will help me?" Katherine could hardly believe her good fortune.

"If I can. I will not call again tomorrow, or it may arouse

suspicion. We may not be able to stop Mistress Douglas being sent to London, but with God's help it may be possible to rescue her *en route*."

"I'm sure that is what my father hopes for," Katherine said anxiously, "but if that is the only way, then it is better than if she has no chance at all. Thank you, Dr Richardson, you have taken a great weight from my shoulders."

They shook hands, and the doctor left. A few minutes later Katherine saw him speaking to her father and Francis outside in the courtyard. The latter did not look too pleased, but eventually they nodded and parted. Ten minutes later Francis called for their horses and they rode off.

Katherine felt jubilant over her victory. Five whole days! Enough time surely for the Royalist sympathizers in the town to be organized. She deliberately did not consider what her punishment would be if her part in it all was discovered. She did not care. She was still sore from the beating, and her shoulders were covered in bruises, but the discomfort was nothing compared to the ache in her heart. For the first time in many months she had begun to pray – not for herself, but for those people who had grown so dear to her in such a short space of time: Barbara and Simon – and Justin – most of all her prayers were for him. Would she ever see him again? She dreaded the thought of the malicious rumour concerning her ever reaching his ears, but forced herself to accept that it was inevitable. By now it was possible he believed her to be not only a liar and a cheat, but directly responsible for the death of his mother and the destruction of his home. It was a bitter pill to swallow, and that night she cried herself to sleep.

The doctor did not come again on the second day as she expected. The medicine he had left was soon half gone and Katherine was afraid her five days of grace would be up before anything had been accomplished. She was still confined to the house, but the restriction on Sarah had been lifted, and on the third morning the girl went to the market square on the pretext of shopping for linen.

During the time she was away Katherine wandered around her rooms in an agony of suspense. After her father had gone out she went along to Barbara's room and found her lying in bed with her eyes tightly closed.

"It's all right – it's me," she said, closing the door behind her, and immediately Barbara sat up. The medicine she had been taking had put a bright feverish flush into her cheeks which had succeeded in convincing Nathaniel Ashley she was not yet well enough to be moved, but he was growing impatient and that greatly worried Katherine.

"Your father came to see me early this morning," Barbara said. "Oliver Cromwell is at Hampton Court. I am to be taken there on Saturday. He made it quite clear that if I still have a fever it will make no difference."

"Saturday – only another two days!" Katherine exclaimed. "With Dr Richardson's help I was hoping for longer."

"Have you seen him again?"

"No – and I am becoming anxious. Sarah has gone out to see if she can pick up any gossip."

"Won't she be followed?"

"I have warned her to be careful. Would you like me to brush your hair?"

"Please. I feel an awful mess. Mother always said I looked more like a tomboy – " Barbara broke off, her face clouding, and Katherine quickly sat down beside her and took her by the hand.

"Please don't be sad."

"I'm frightened, Katherine. Will I ever see Justin or Simon again?"

"Yes, of course you will. It is impossible for me to get you out of the house, but Dr Richardson has friends who will make sure you never reach Hampton Court. In less than a week I am sure you will be safely on your way to France with your brothers."

"I wish you could come with me."

"I wish it too, but it is impossible," Katherine replied quietly.

Sarah came into the bedroom as Katherine finished curling Barbara's long brown hair. She was out of breath and obviously agitated.

"Mistress Katherine, they've been seen – " she began.

"Come in and close the door, Sarah. Do you want the whole house to hear you?" Katherine interrupted. "Now, sit down and tell us, slowly, what has happened."

"The King . . . at least everyone thinks it was him . . . "

"Well?"

"He was seen this morning travelling south."

Barbara started up, a hand against her throat, asking anxiously: "Was anyone with him?"

"Two men."

"Thank God." She turned to Katherine, tears in her eyes. "Justin and Simon."

"The Major has fifty men riding after them," Sarah said, her eyes on her mistress's ashen face. "He's making ready to leave himself, but he won't catch them."

"I pray you are right," Katherine whispered. She leaned against the bedpost behind her, seized with a sudden fit of trembling. Justin alive and with the King! The news made her feel faint with relief. If they reached the coast safely and could find a ship, they could be at sea before the troopers ever arrived. He would not have risked the open road without some definite plan in mind.

"Is there any other gossip, Sarah?"

"Only the usual tittle-tattle, mistress. I did see Dr Richardson, though, and he bade me tell you the matter you discussed has been taken care of."

"But why did he not call again?"

"The Major sent a message telling him his services are no longer required as his patient is better."

"No matter." Katherine's face brightened. "We are not forsaken, Barbara – " she began, then abruptly broke off as the door opened without warning and Nathaniel Ashley's frame blocked the doorway. He surveyed the three women with a humourless smile.

"I see you have heard the news. I am leaving now, Katherine. You will make no attempt to leave the house while I am away, and there are guards posted outside to ensure our guest also remains. She may have company on her journey."

"You will never catch my brothers," Barbara said coldly.

"The reward for the capture of the fugitives Charles and Justin Douglas has been raised by a further hundred pounds for each man. I know men who would betray their own mothers for such money."

"How proud that must make you, Father," Katherine said contemptuously. "However, there are still men who cannot be bought, who still risk their lives out of loyalty – sometimes love, neither of which you will ever comprehend."

"You are in no position to spit fire at me, girl. Do you need reminding that only I stand between you and prison? I have shielded you thus far, but do not provoke me further or I might withdraw my protection. While I am away you would be better employed in prayer than in treasonous talk with the sister of a traitor."

The door slammed shut behind him and Katherine stood silent for a long while, her hands clenched tightly at her sides.

"Don't argue with him, or he'll take a stick to you again," Sarah pleaded.

"He – he hasn't beaten you, has he?" Barbara asked, her eyes wide with horror.

"Yes."

"But why? Did he think you could tell him where the King was?"

"That was one reason. His main aim was to cleanse my soul of impurities."

"By beating you? I suppose he quoted passages from the Bible to ease your pain."

"Yes – as a matter of fact he did. That's his way. The terrible thing is he doesn't realize what he has become."

"My father never once struck me, nor can I remember him ever hitting Justin or Simon either. He said if it ever became necessary to resort to such methods we would lose all respect for him, and striking us would not bring it back."

"He was right. I have no respect for my father – or love."

"I wish Justin was here. He would know what to do."

"I will do whatever is necessary to free you from my father," Katherine assured her.

"But afterwards? I am afraid for you."

"Afterwards does not matter."

Katherine returned to her room and tried to rest before dinner. She had slept very little since her return to Newbury, and the lack of rest was beginning to take its toll of both her strength and nerves, but her mind was so disturbed that she found it impossible to relax, and the appearance of Francis Grahaeme did nothing to ease the mounting anxiety inside her. He halted beside her chair, pulling on his thick riding gloves. Her heart racing, she realized he too was leaving. That left only the guards.

"I have been ordered to Reading to meet Lord Cromwell, Katherine. He requires a personal account of the King's activities in this area."

"How important you have become to have the ear of the great man himself," she returned coldly.

"He trusts my judgment. There was another letter with my orders. My appointment to his personal staff." A sardonic smile twisted Francis's mouth. He looked very pleased with himself and that unnerved her. The new position would give him the power he craved – more power than her father held – more influence over her if he so chose. "I thought perhaps you might have something to say to me."

"I will never beg, Francis." She understood his meaning immediately. Marriage or exposure and the threat of being arrested for her part in the King's escape.

"No? Think on it while I am away," was his parting remark.

Katherine puzzled over his words for many hours. Did he mean to omit her from his report and hold it over her head as blackmail? Until he returned his words would torture her mind; perhaps it was his way of punishing her for refusing his offer of marriage.

The guards on the ground floor did not invade her privacy, knowing there was no other way out of the house, and she took advantage of her father's absence to go down to the library late that same night. She had been lying in bed for hours, unable to sleep, listening to the sounds of the sentries patrolling outside. As a clock somewhere in the house chimed twelve she pulled a robe over her nightgown and stole down to the lower floor. The library was unusually cold and she was surprised to see the curtains billowing out through the open french windows. The windows opened out onto a small veranda with some steps leading down to the gardens. It was possible her father had not fastened them, but more likely that one of the troopers had taken the opportunity to come in and rest in more comfortable surroundings, she mused as she moved across the room.

A figure stepped out from behind the heavy drapes on one side of her. It was too dark to distinguish his face but there was sufficient light for her to see the sword-blade menacing her. She stepped back in alarm, a scream rising in her throat. It never materialized, for she was roughly seized from the rear. A cloth was tied across her mouth and her arms were held behind her, stilling her struggles.

"I warned you that if you ever betrayed me I would come back and take care of you personally," Justin said, in a low, harsh whisper.

CHAPTER EIGHT

KATHERINE'S relief at finding it was Justin and Simon who had broken into the house was short-lived. The sight of Justin's glittering eyes made her feel instantly afraid. She shook her head and made incoherent noises beneath the gag, trying to convey she was innocent of the rumours he had heard, but he remained unmoved.

"No, Kate. I'll not fall foul of your witchery again," he said coldly. He turned to his brother, who had slipped out of the library to explore. "Well?"

"There are two guards below, but otherwise the house seems deserted. Her room must be above," Simon said, looking at Katherine. His voice, too, was cold and unfriendly, and her heart sank. They had sought her out believing the worst. Had they been back to the gutted house and found their mother's grave?

"Take her upstairs then," Justin ordered, "and if she is troublesome, knock her out, but don't kill her. That pleasure should be mine."

The murmur of voices came to them as Simon pulled Katherine out after him into the corridor. She offered no resistance, frightened not just by Justin's threat, but by the thought of their being seen by one of the guards. It was not until the door of her bedroom had been closed and locked that she was able to see her two companions clearly, and then her horrified gaze took in, not only their travel-stained clothes and bearded faces, but the ominous red patch on the front of Justin's jacket. Even as she stared at him he stumbled back against the bed and collapsed across it with a groan of pain.

"Find something to pad this wound – I'm bleeding like a stuck pig," he muttered.

Simon dragged open the nearest drawer, pulled out one of the petticoats there and began to tear it into strips. Unfastening the cloth around her mouth, Katherine knelt at the side of the bed and reached for Justin's jacket, but he pulled away from her with an oath:

"Keep your distance!"

"Let me help you," she pleaded.

"As you helped my mother?" His face was twisted with anger and grief as he lifted his sword until the tip of it touched Katherine's breast. The locket she wore swam before his tortured vision and his hand began to shake. "She helped you when you were hurt – she liked you and you repaid her with a bullet."

"I had no part in it, Justin. You must believe me. Captain Grahaeme killed her when she tried to escape. I saw it happen."

"I swore I would kill you if you betrayed me or mine."

"Then kill me. It will only take a little thrust for that blade to enter my body. Surely you have the strength for that, Justin. Why do you hesitate?" Bright tears flooded into Katherine's eyes and welled unchecked down over her cheeks, but she did not move and her challenging gaze never left Justin's face. "I would gladly have given my own life to save her, and that's the truth."

Justin's pain-ravaged features glazed before her blurred vision. Without a sound he fell back onto the pillows and lay still.

Simon glared at her across his brother's unconscious form.

"Bind his wound, and if you so much as look towards the door or window I'll save him the trouble of killing you."

Easing off Justin's jacket, Katherine cut away the blood-soaked shirt and washed and dressed the ugly wound in his side. Simon retrieved his knife as soon as she had finished and pushed it back into his belt. He inspected the sparsely furnished sitting-room, locked the outside door and then came back to where she was trying to pull the sheets from beneath Justin's inert form.

"Please help me and then go and gather up everything that is bloodstained. Sarah will have to burn it all before it is seen."

"Where is Sarah?" Simon asked, and she noticed a sudden change in his tone. She had forgotten the relationship which had developed between them.

"In bed. Where else would she be at this hour? My father will be away from the house for at least a day, so you have no need to stand there with your sword drawn. Captain Grahaeme is away also and you are in no danger from me."

"Justin thinks otherwise and I am inclined to agree with him. He came here to kill you – at least that's what he told me." Sheathing his weapon Simon caught her by the wrist, his young face pale and set. "How did my mother die? She went to warn you when Justin said you had left the lodge and gone off on your own."

"Did he say why?"

"No – I guessed you had quarrelled. He won't talk about it."

"No more will I. What happened between us is private. I did leave the lodge and I went in the wrong direction. I found the look-out you had posted dying on the hill. I ran back to try and warn Justin, but he was gone and by the time I reached the house ..." Katherine closed her eyes for a moment and knew he could feel her trembling at the memory of what she had seen. "The house was ablaze. Barbara was a prisoner and your mother ... she was shot when she tried to run away."

"By this Captain Grahaeme?"

"Yes. In the morning we came here. Barbara is a prisoner here – she is to be taken to Cromwell the day after tomorrow."

"Our friends in the town tell a different story," Simon interposed, and the fingers circling her wrist tightened ominously.

"My father's way of protecting himself," Katherine returned. "Ask Sarah – ask your own sister. Look round you, if you don't believe me. I have defied my father, rejected all the things he believes in, and because of it he has deprived me of everything I hold dear. Until I renounce Justin this is how I must live – in these empty shells, as much a prisoner as your sister."

Simon released her and turned to look at his unconscious brother, clearly agitated by her words.

"Is Barbara's room on this floor?"

"Yes. Oh, Simon, why did you come here? Her escape has all been arranged."

"So we were led to believe. Dr Richardson is the most loyal man we have in these parts," Simon returned with a tight smile. "He arranged to have your father and the troopers decoyed away on Justin's orders."

"And the King?"

"Safe. Miles from here. When we have Barbara we will take ship for France. That's if Justin can make it," he added with a worried frown.

Katherine pulled up a chair beside the bed and sat down, her eyes riveted on Justin's bearded face. He looked as if he had not eaten for days. Without thinking she reached out and touched the thick black hair and the rough, unshaven cheeks. How she longed to lean down and kiss him, assure him of her loyalty and her love.

"A touching gesture." Simon stood beside her, his expression guarded. "To convince me you are genuine perhaps?"

"Once you believed in me." Katherine allowed his bitterness to flow over her.

"And my mother died, Barbara is a prisoner and Justin – he's half dead from loss of blood. I trusted you when he did not. It seems he is wiser than I am."

"I have told you the truth," Katherine returned quietly. She was over the first shock of seeing them now. Her composure was returning and with it the knowledge they had placed not only themselves in danger, but Barbara too. With guards below and outside and Justin wounded, she had no idea how they could get out of the house unseen. There was also Francis Grahaeme to be reckoned with if he returned unexpectedly.

"I cannot afford to believe you again," Simon said. Picking up the remnants of her petticoat, he ripped a long piece of material from it and proceeded to tie her hands behind her to the chair. Gagging her, he quietly unlocked the door and stepped out into the corridor, leaving Katherine to sit alone by the bed and helplessly watch Justin's restless movements – unable to comfort him in any way or shut her ears against his feverish ramblings.

It seemed an eternity before Simon returned, bringing his sister with him. Barbara began to protest at the sight of her bound friend, but he waved her to silence and, crossing to the chair, grasped the front of Katherine's robe and pulled it down over her shoulders. On both arms and along her back dark bruises stood out on the whiteness of her smooth skin.

"My God! Your father did this?" he demanded, and when Katherine nodded he hurriedly rearranged her robe and freed her from her bonds. "Forgive me, Katherine – to have treated you so roughly after that . . . I am deeply ashamed."

"With so much at stake you were right not to trust me." Katherine smiled at Barbara, knowing she had told Simon everything. "Thank you."

"Is Justin badly hurt?" Barbara bent over her brother, bravely trying to hold back the tears. Katherine guessed she had never seen him hurt before and that it alarmed her. Justin had been the strong one, never ill, never worried, never vulnerable, and now he lay before her completely powerless to give her the comfort she so desperately needed.

"He is very weak," Katherine said gently. She met Simon's questioning gaze and shook her head, indicating he could not be moved, but not to alarm his sister. "You look tired, Simon, why don't you rest on the couch in the other room?"

"I think I will."

"I will stay here," Barbara said firmly, but Katherine drew her away from the bed.

"There is nothing you or any of us can do until morning. I want you to go back to bed and try to sleep. Tomorrow, with Sarah's help, I think I may be able to get Dr Richardson to attend Justin."

"How?" Barbara's face immediately brightened. Of course Katherine would find an answer! She was as level-headed as Justin.

"We will talk when you have had some sleep. Go back to

your room now. I must go down to the library and close the windows," Katherine said to Simon as soon as she had seen Barbara safely back to her room.

"Then what?" Simon asked quietly.

"I will stay here." Katherine motioned to the chair behind her.

"You do realize the risk you are taking, don't you?" Simon asked, a frown furrowing his fair brows. "If I wasn't so damned tired I'd drag both Justin and Barbara out of here and we would take our chance on the road. With the Major and his men miles away we'd have a small chance at least."

"Justin could not stay on a horse for more than half a mile – if that. If I can get Dr Richardson here tomorrow I may be able to arrange transport of some kind for all of you, and you will be away from here before my father returns," Katherine replied. Already a wild idea was forming in her mind, but so much depended on the doctor being allowed back into the house and Francis Grahaeme staying away from her. His attentions would be disastrous now.

Throughout the remaining hours of darkness, while Simon slept soundly in the sitting-room and Justin slept, less peacefully, under Katherine's watchful eye, she sat by the bed, holding tightly to one of his hands. She dozed towards morning, but was awakened by the sentries changing outside her window and knew it to be eight o'clock.

Justin appeared more restful, but his colour had not improved, and from time to time he mumbled incoherently. Once he opened his eyes and stared up at her, but did not know her. By the time Sarah brought her breakfast, Katherine was fully dressed and had replaced the bandages on Justin's wound, which were spotted with fresh blood. She turned away from the sight of her maid in Simon's arms, remembering how wonderful it had been with Justin. She would never know the like of it again.

She turned as someone lightly touched her shoulder and found herself looking into Simon's sympathetic face.

"I'm a tactless oaf," he muttered. "My only excuse is that I feel about her as you feel about Justin."

Katherine's eyes widened. She had not realized it was as serious as that.

"Then you must take her with you."

"She refuses to leave without you. Come with us, Katherine, please."

"If my plan is to succeed, I have to remain behind." Katherine moved away, motioning to the tray of food Sarah had brought. "Are you hungry?"

"Ravenous."

"Then sit down and eat as much as you like. Sarah, gather up these bloodstained bandages and take them into Barbara's room. May I borrow your knife, Simon?"

Mystified, he handed it to her.

"Thank you. Lock this door behind us and don't come out, no matter what you hear, but unlock the sitting-room door for me," Katherine said firmly.

Barbara was sitting up in bed staring in bewilderment at the bandages Sarah had placed on the end of the bed. Katherine smiled at them both and proceeded to unfold the idea she had worked out the night before.

The guards were about to sit down to breakfast in the kitchen when a shrill scream brought them leaping to their feet, reaching for their pistols. A dishevelled, wide-eyed Sarah met them half way up the stairs.

"Up there – upstairs!" She collapsed, sobbing, against the wall. "Hurry – oh God! She's dying!"

The troopers went up the stairs two at a time. They were not sure whether she meant the Major's daughter or the Royalist prisoner, but for anything to happen to either of them would mean a very uncomfortable time with their commanding officer when he returned. Mistakes were not allowed.

The door at the far end of the passage was wide open, and through it Katherine could be seen bending over the prostrate figure of Barbara Douglas, sprawled across the bed. The cloth she was pressing against the unconscious girl's breast was covered in blood.

"No! Don't touch her! She mustn't be moved!" Katherine

cried out sharply as the two men came out of their shocked stupor and moved towards the bed. "I've sent for the doctor. She tried to kill herself with a knife. She must have had it with her all the time. One of you go and hurry the doctor."

Katherine bent lower over Barbara, partly shielding her from the curious eyes of the remaining trooper. He turned away, his gaze taking in the bloodstains streaked across the bedcovers and the slim-bladed dagger, the tip still red, lying on the floor. Picking it up he put it carefully to one side. He was older than his companion and not so easily swayed by the sight of a woman's tearful face, Katherine realized, but then additional support arrived in the shape of Dr Richardson. At a single glance he took in Katherine leaning across the apparently unconscious form of Barbara Douglas, the bloodstains and the hard-faced trooper who appeared about to investigate further. On Katherine's instructions Sarah had told him all there was to know on the way to the house, and he acted promptly.

"You" – he wheeled on Sarah, hovering in the doorway – "bring me clean towels and hot water and take these men with you."

"I will remain, doctor," the older man insisted.

Dr Richardson snapped open his bag and glared at him from beneath shaggy brows.

"I have no intention of treating this young woman half naked under your nose, sir. I would remind you she is a valuable prisoner and you are delaying my treatment of her."

"Then I will wait outside the door for your report."

"I care not where you wait so long as it is not in my sight. Trouble me again and I will report you to the Major. Mistress Ashley – help me lift the poor child onto the pillows," the doctor muttered, ignoring his unwelcome onlooker. When he glanced up the trooper had withdrawn and the door was closed. He looked across at Katherine with a tight smile. "The thought of your father's retribution is indeed a strong deterrent. How will you fare when he discovers this farce?"

She shrugged her shoulders. At that moment it was the least of her worries.

"No worse than I already have. Thank you for coming so

promptly. Another moment and I am sure that man would have discovered the trick."

"How did you manage the blood?" Dr Richardson asked. He did not look up from his task of bandaging Barbara's shoulder. Inquisitive eyes would have to be satisfied – even for the short while she was to remain in the house.

"Most of the bandages came from Sir Justin. He is very weak, doctor. He will need help to leave here."

"That is already being arranged. The difficulty will be in getting them out of the house. How will you manage it?"

"The escape will have to be made through the gardens. If you could have some kind of a conveyance waiting in the small road on the far side – they would have a good chance."

"There – that should convince our suspicious friend outside." Dr Richardson stood back and regarded Barbara, who lay still and quiet, her eyes firmly closed. "I suggest you remain that way, young lady."

"She will, I assure you. Not only her own life, but those of her brothers depend on it. You knew they were coming here, doctor?"

"They came to me first. I have been a friend of the family for many years. The rumours spread by your father did not place you in a very good light in their eyes. Sir Justin especially seemed determined to believe the worst of you. I told him how much you had risked in order to help his sister, but he placed the worst misconstruction on my words, saying you were trying to trick your way back into her confidence in order to find out if she knew the whereabouts of the King. It is not like him to be so unreasonable."

"If you knew what had gone before you would understand his attitude," Katherine said. Her voice was unsteady and she began to sway, at the same time clutching at her left forearm. "I feel a little faint, doctor, would you mind helping me back to my room?"

The soldier standing outside turned inquiringly as the doctor came out of the bedroom, his arm round Katherine's waist. Sarah followed with his bag. He looked beyond them to the bed and the motionless girl lying there.

"The wound is not serious. If she is allowed to rest she will be able to travel when the Major wishes," Dr Richardson informed him, and moved on before he could be questioned further.

"He's suspicious enough to put a guard outside," he said, closing the door of Katherine's sitting-room behind them.

"No matter. I will deal with him when the time comes." She turned the key silently in the lock and drew him away towards the bedroom.

"As efficiently as you took care to ensure there was fresh blood on the knife Mistress Douglas is supposed to have used," the doctor said in a quiet tone. "Let me see your arm."

Wordlessly Katherine obeyed. He pulled back her sleeve to reveal a narrow cut about two inches long along her forearm. It had bled profusely when she had first inflicted it with Simon's dagger, enabling her to make Barbara's suicide attempt more convincing. Now it was beginning to throb madly, and the pain made her feel quite faint.

"Please see to Justin first. Mine is only a scratch."

Dr Richardson straightened, his eyes filled with unspoken admiration.

"How you must love him. Where is he?"

"In there." Katherine motioned towards the bedroom. As she spoke the communicating door slowly opened and Simon emerged. Seeing they were alone he pushed the pistol he held into his belt and stood back for them to enter.

"Sit down," Dr Richardson ordered Katherine.

Taking some bandages from his bag he held them out to Sarah.

"Use this to bind your mistress's arm and then find more – Sir Justin's wound will need a heavy dressing if he is to travel."

Katherine sank down into the nearest chair as her legs gave way beneath her. A moment later Simon was beside her, pushing a cushion beneath her head, and then Sarah was gently winding the bandage around her arm.

"I had my ear pressed to the door – I heard every word," he said in a low, fierce whisper. "Are you mad, Katherine? You have made it impossible not to be implicated in Barbara's escape. You will go to Hampton Court in her place. Have you considered that?"

"Yes. There was no other way – Justin needed a doctor."

"He also needs you. I insist you come with us."

"No."

"Because of what passed between you at the lodge?"

"Yes."

"Was it so terrible?"

"Please, Simon, I don't want to talk about it. Justin doesn't care for me, and I will never allow him to be burdened with me out of gratitude – or pity."

"When I tell him all you have done for us . . . "

"He will feel obliged to me – nothing more." Tentatively Katherine got up and went across to the chest of drawers from which she took another petticoat and proceeded to tear it into strips. Simon helped her in silence, obviously disturbed by the fierce love which drove her to such extremes to protect his brother yet which was destined to be smothered because of a stupid misunderstanding.

"When will it be safe to move him?" he asked at length.

Dr Richardson looked up at him, then inquiringly at Katherine.

"When will the Major return?"

"Once he discovers he has been following the wrong men he will return at once. He could be home by morning."

"Then I will make the arrangements for tonight. I will leave a sleeping draught with you. Give it to Sir Justin no later than seven o'clock."

"Is that necessary?" Katherine asked, aghast.

"He must be kept quiet at all costs. If he is restless, gag him. How will you get him out to the road?"

"I will carry him," Simon answered. "With my sister's help, we will manage."

"Sarah and I will be there too. Yes, we will manage," Katherine added determinedly.

"For all our sakes, I hope so," the doctor said. "How will you explain this to your father?"

"The soldiers are convinced Barbara is hurt. I see no reason why I should tell him otherwise. It will explain your reason for being here and you will not be implicated," Katherine replied. She had been over it all very carefully in her mind and knew exactly what she would say when the time came. "While my father was away, Simon and Justin came for her – overpowered the guards and took her. He will know I aided them, but that does not matter. I have not tried to hide the way I feel about Justin."

Simon heard the tremor in her voice and silently cursed the ill luck which kept his brother from hearing it also and realizing the great wrong he had done her.

"Very well. At midnight then. What time does the watch change?"

"Not until eight the following morning, by which time they will be miles from here, God willing," Katherine said, and a smile touched her tired features at the thought. "Is there anything more we can do, doctor?"

"Only rest. It will be a long night for us all."

After Dr Richardson had left the house, Sarah went down to the kitchen on the pretext of fetching some warm broth for her mistress, who was feeling unwell after the unpleasantness of the morning. She returned with the news that a fresh trooper had been placed outside Barbara's door and that another had ridden in all haste to the Major to bring him back to the house.

"The sergeant does not trust you," Simon said, looking at Katherine with anxious eyes.

"He has good reason. He was present when I told my father how much I despised him – and myself – for the way we lived. He knows I was connected with Justin and the King and is probably watching me as closely as he is Barbara, but there is nothing he can do until my father returns, and by then you will all be gone."

Taking the bowl of broth from Sarah, she sat beside the bed and moistened Justin's dry lips with a little of the liquid. A few hours later, with Simon supporting him, she managed to get him to take a little nourishment, but immediately afterwards he again lapsed into a semi-conscious state without knowing who tended him so painstakingly.

Simon and Sarah moved the couch from the sitting-room into a corner of the bedroom and sat together, keeping their voices low so as not to be heard by any sharp ears outside the door or disturb Katherine who kept a constant vigil at Justin's side. From time to time Katherine turned to look at them, arms about each other. Before, the sight had troubled her, but now she was pleased they had been able to spend at least a short while together, secure in the knowledge that their love was steadfast. No matter how long Sarah had to wait, Katherine believed she would remain true to the young Royalist who had stolen her heart; it was in her nature, as it was also in Katherine's.

An incoherent mutter from the bed brought her attention back to Justin. His eyes were open, clear of fever, but shadowed with pain and weariness.

"You!" His voice was weak, but she heard the note of incredulity as he recognized her, and watched it creep into the expression on his face as he slowly turned his head and saw the two lovers on the couch. "What the devil . . . !"

"Don't talk. You will need your strength," Katherine whispered.

"Don't give me orders, Kate." The dark eyes glared at her with no spark of friendliness in them. She quickly stood up as hot tears rushed to her eyes, and called Simon over, afraid Justin would over-excite himself if she remained at his side.

"He must be made to rest and and he will not listen to me," she said through trembling lips.

"But he will to me."

"You are not to discuss me or anything that has happened in this house since you arrived," she said sharply, and although Simon looked stubborn, he did not argue.

Katherine left them and shut herself in the sitting-room and there, alone in the darkness, she gave way to her tears.

As was her custom, whenever she was alone in the house, Katherine took all her meals in her rooms, waited on only by Sarah. That evening, after Katherine had rejoined the others, the maid brought her usual supper tray and reported that the servants, although they were speculating wildly on what had happened that morning, had in no way connected Katherine with the incident. If anything, they felt concerned for the terrible shock she had received and understood her natural desire to remain closeted in her rooms.

"What about the sergeant?"

"He is having his food in the kitchen, but the other trooper is still outside Mistress Barbara's room." Sarah delved deep into her pockets and brought out two lean ham hocks wrapped in a clean handkerchief, an apple and a freshly baked meat pie. "You have not eaten all day – you need your supper. This will suffice for Simon. There's extra milk on the tray and more broth for Sir Justin."

"You are a marvellous girl," Simon chuckled, reaching for one of the ham hocks. "What about my sister?"

"I looked in earlier, but I was watched so closely I dared not speak to her," Sarah answered. "I pretended she was still sleeping, and told him not to disturb her any more tonight."

"Barbara – what has happened to her?" Justin raised his head and stared across at them. He looked stronger after his sleep, Katherine thought. Once more on the defensive against her.

"Nothing at all, Justin. She is pretending to be ill, to fool the soldiers, that's all," Simon assured him.

Justin turned his accusing gaze on Katherine and struggled to sit up, but he was restrained by his brother and lay back on the pillows, fighting for breath.

"You are not to trust her. Do you hear me, boy?"

"Simon is quite capable of making up his own mind." Katherine ignored his daggered glare and sat down on the edge of the bed, holding the bowl of broth. "Please be still and let me feed you, or you will not be strong enough to travel."

Justin looked questioningly at Simon, who nodded.

"Tonight. Dr Richardson has arranged it all – without his help we would have been discovered long ago. And without Katherine's quick intervention, you would surely have died.

It was she who brought the doctor here by pretending Barbara needed him."

"Let him eat, Simon," Katherine protested, embarrassed by his protestations on her behalf. She knew he wanted to exonerate her from the rumour Justin believed, and smiled at him gratefully, showing him she understood. With a shrug he moved away and allowed her to feed his brother without interruption.

"Stay, I don't want you out of my sight," Justin said as she rose to go. The lean fingers which encircled her wrist were surprisingly strong, and she sat down again, motioning Sarah to take away the empty bowl. The maid looked across at Simon, at a loss to understand Katherine's calmness. Moments later they saw Justin's eyes close and his grip on her slacked. Gently she freed herself and stood up with a soft sigh.

"I put the sleeping draught Dr Richardson gave me into the broth," she said simply. "I'm sorry, Simon, but he was going to be difficult. This way it will be all over by the time he recovers."

"And you will not have to give him an explanation." Simon returned with a frown. "What are you afraid of, Katherine?"

She stared at him for a long while, bright tears glistening in her eyes. How could she explain the pain of being scorned – of knowing that the man she loved would never love her? It was impossible!

"We will go downstairs fifteen minutes before midnight," she said quietly. "That will give us enough time to get Justin out through the gardens. Five minutes before that you and I will take care of the guard outside Barbara's room, Simon. I will help her get dressed and then bring her back here. Until then I suggest we try to rest."

CHAPTER NINE

Lack of sleep caught up with Katherine as she sat in her chair, and she dozed without realizing it until Simon awakened her at the prearranged time. Between them they replaced Justin's boots and outer clothing and then began to put into operation the plan they had discussed earlier.

Unlocking the door, Katherine stepped out into the corridor and went along to Barbara's room. The light from the single candle she carried was enough to guide her footsteps and illuminate her features for the guard, but not sufficiently for him to see the man who kept to the shadow some feet behind her.

"I am worried about Mistress Douglas," she told the tired-eyed soldier, who blinked at her in surprise. "Will you please open the door so that I may see her before I retire for the night?"

Although somewhat taken aback by her arrival, the man did as she asked. Katherine put down the candle on a table and bent over the bed. A moment later she said:

"It is very dark in here. Will you be good enough to bring more light?"

The butt of Simon's pistol struck the man's head from behind as he moved into the room. Barbara sat up with a startled gasp as Katherine helped to drag him into a corner.

"I'll tie him up while you get dressed," Simon said to her. "Quickly now, this is no time for modesty."

She jumped out of bed, and with Katherine's help was fully dressed in a matter of minutes. The unconscious soldier, tied and securely gagged, was deposited in the bed and covered with the bedclothes. The house was quiet and still in darkness as they stole back to where Sarah anxiously waited.

"That was the easy part," Simon muttered, looking down at Justin. His brother was no light weight.

"Will it help if we all try to carry him?" Barbara asked.

"No, that would make too much noise. Katherine, here – you take Justin's pistol. Go first and make sure the way is clear. Barbara, you will follow as soon as she reaches the library, then I will bring Justin, and Sarah will come last."

Katherine waited for a moment on the landing, listening for some sound from below, but the only noise she could hear was the loud thudding of her own heart. She slipped down the stairs, keeping close to the banister rail in order to see any sudden light from below, and silently swung open the library door. After drawing the curtains across the windows she stood by the door. One by one the others came down. First Barbara, cautiously feeling her way, then Simon with the unconscious Justin slumped over his shoulder and, close behind, a watchful Sarah. Katherine closed and locked the door and forced a smile to her drawn features as she turned to face them.

"Rest a moment."

Simon shook his head. Justin's weight was obviously a great strain, and she nodded understandingly.

The garden was bright with moonlight as she opened the windows and stepped out, her gaze sweeping over the well-tended lawns in front of her. There were another two soldiers to be accounted for. One would be at the front of the house – but where was the other? Asleep somewhere perhaps – or watching her from the trees, waiting to see her next move.

"You are up late, Mistress Ashley."

She spun round with a startled cry to find herself face to face with the sergeant who had stepped out of the shadows beyond the trees. She felt herself begin to tremble beneath the suspicious gaze which raked her from head to toe.

"I could not sleep. It has been an upsetting day." Somehow she managed to keep her voice steady. The feel of the pistol in the hand she held behind her back was reassuring.

"That it has. I have no doubt the Major will also find it upsetting. Come, mistress, I will escort you back to your room before I look in on our guest. I would not like anything to happen to either of you before the Major returns in the morning."

His sarcasm was not lost on Katherine. He did suspect her! Thank goodness she had Justin's pistol. Bringing her hand from behind her skirts she levelled it at him and cocked it:

"Please do not make me shoot you."

"You little fool! Give that to me."

"No."

"The noise of a shot will bring more of my men," the sergeant sneered. "What chance of an escape then, eh?"

"None perhaps," Katherine returned calmly, "but you would be deprived of the pleasure of seeing me taken because you would be dead." She stepped back, motioning him to enter the library. He stepped past, cursing her under his breath, and met with the same fate as the upstairs guard.

Katherine leaned against the window, trembling violently, but by the time Sarah and Barbara had secured the man with curtain cords, she had overcome her moment of weakness. As silent as the shadows round them, they crossed the lawn and entered the trees. The road was on the far side of the gardens and Simon's strength was gone before it was reached. They rested for a brief moment, then went on with Sarah leading the way and the others supporting Justin between them.

On the other side of a small wicket gate stood a wagon piled high with hay. Katherine helped Barbara through a mist of tears to cover Justin while Simon and Sarah said their farewells.

"Bless you for all you have done." Simon took Katherine's hand in his. His voice was very unsteady and then, to her amazement, he went down on one knee before her and touched her fingers with his lips in a reverent gesture.

"Please – don't," she entreated. "Go now before I weep all over you. Take care of Justin for me."

"You know I will. As soon as he is able to listen he will hear the truth."

"No. You must promise me to say nothing of my part in this until you are safely in France," Katherine whispered in sudden alarm. "Do you think I have risked so much, so many lives, to have him come back for me and be captured?"

"So you think he would come back! Then he must care for you – and if he does, nothing on earth could prevent him returning."

"You can – by remaining silent. Give me your word, Simon."

"Very well, you have it. God keep you, Katherine."

"And you – all of you."

She pulled herself free and stepped away from him, tears streaming down her cheeks. The wheels of the cart had been bound with strips of cloth so that when it moved away there would be little or no sound. Katherine realized she had not asked where they were to go, and then was glad she had not. If she did not know, she could not be made to betray them into enemy hands.

"Oh, mistress, will we ever see them again?" Sarah came to her side; she too was crying.

"Not until Charles sits on the throne of England – if that day ever comes," Katherine replied quietly. "You are not to be sad, but thankful they are on their way to safety. Perhaps you should have gone too."

"And leave you to face the Major alone? How could you think I would do such a thing? But I can't help being afraid, Mistress Katherine. When he finds out Sir Justin was here . . . the King's Shadow himself . . . "

A shadow detached itself from the trees in front of them, materializing into the outline of a man. The pistol held in one hand and levelled at Simon, who stood immobile with shock, was clearly visible in the bright moonlight. Sarah clapped her hands over her mouth to suppress a scream as the mocking tones of Francis Grahaeme came out of the darkness.

"Yes, Katherine, what have you planned to do when he finds out? Throw yourself on his mercy? You know you will get none. Brazen it out and take the consequences? Foolish bravery and such a waste of time and effort. Be still, my friend, very still, or I will put a bullet through your sister's very pretty head." The last threatening words were directed at Simon who was cautiously edging closer, and the pistol was deliberately turned on Barbara who was standing beside the hay cart where Justin lay unconscious beneath a protective covering of hay.

"He means it – keep still," Katherine begged.

"I remember you," Simon muttered, "from the inn ... Katherine said you were the one who led the attack on my home, murdered my mother ... " His eyes began to blaze with such fury that Katherine feared he might throw himself on the other man, and caught him tightly by the arm.

"Don't be provoked ... he isn't alone. Where are your men, Francis? Hiding in the trees, waiting for us to run perhaps so that you can shoot us in the back too? How long have you been watching us?"

"Since you reached the road. You had the devil's own luck in avoiding the guards – or have you killed them?"

"No." Katherine was disgusted at the calmness with which he spoke of death. Her eyes searched the darkness beyond him, but she could see no one else, hear no sound. There was no way of telling how many muskets were levelled at them.

"Unfortunate. I would have left no witnesses to my actions."

"I do not find it as easy as you to kill innocent people." Katherine was remembering the death of Justin's mother as she spoke, and her voice was full of bitterness.

"I have learned how pleasant life can be – whereas, it seems, you have not, or you would not be eager to throw yours away." As Francis began to move slowly in the direction of the cart Katherine felt Simon's muscles tense beneath her hand and tightened her grasp warningly. The pistol was still aimed at Barbara, and she knew he would not hesitate to use it. Pulling aside the hay which was spread across Justin's inert form, he glanced down at him and she heard a deep chuckle rise in his throat. "Is this your famous King's Shadow? Faith, he looks like a half-starved peasant. And wounded too. What protection can he offer you now, Katherine?"

"Let them go, Francis."

"Don't grovel to him," Simon muttered fiercely. "Call your men and let us be done with this play-acting. My brother is in need of help."

"I believe he is alone." Katherine moved away from Simon, watching Francis's face as she spoke. She saw the eyes narrow only slightly, but it was sufficient to prove her suspicions were correct. A wild idea was beginning to race through her brain. As a low moan came from the direction of the cart she was prompted into action. "If you are not alone, Francis, why have you waited so long to arrest us? Call your men – let them be witnesses to this moment of triumph. What an achievement to crown your new appointment! Cromwell will be proud of you, and so will my father when he returns. The man who captured the King's Shadow ... under the circumstances your past indiscretions may be overlooked. Of course it will not be the same as being a family man ... with a wife ... "

"Katherine, what in the world are you talking about?" Simon interrupted.

"Francis understands me perfectly." Katherine sensed the indecision going through Francis's mind, although she suspected the idea could have been with him ever since he discovered the escape. Why else had he not raised the alarm? He was greedy and ambitious. He wanted Katherine as his wife and the coveted position with Oliver Cromwell. The two things could not be separated if he was to remain in favour, protected by a cloak of respectability. "Let them go. I would be grateful."

"No! How can you speak of such a thing when you love Justin?" Barbara cried out, clearly distressed by the implication.

"Don't you understand it is because I love him? Well, Francis?" How controlled she sounded – thank goodness he could not see into her heart and the terrible fear there. What if the capture of the King's Shadow meant more prestige than his new appointment?

"You will marry me?" His voice was completely without emotion, but his eyes blazed with what she could only suppose was excitement. He had always professed he wanted her, but she had never really believed him. Had he spoken the truth after all? The thought that he might care for her made her feel momentarily faint, and she swayed unsteadily.

"Katherine – in Justin's name, I forbid this." Simon's voice came to her from a long way off.

"Yes, Francis, I will marry you if you allow my friends to go free and promise me not to send anyone after them . . . "

"Until it becomes necessary – which will be in the morning when the escape of Mistress Douglas is discovered. That is all the time I can give them. Very well, Katherine, I agree to your terms."

By his confident tone she knew she had been right and that this was what he had been hoping for all along. Neither Simon, nor Justin, even Barbara, meant anything to him. Uppermost in his mind was his promotion, secure now he was to marry the daughter of a respected army major. She could have cried with relief.

"Take Justin and go." She turned on Simon appealingly. "Think only of yourselves from now on."

"Into the cart before I change my mind!" Francis strode across the space between them and caught Katherine by the wrist, dragging her away from the other man. Without a word Simon obeyed, but the expression on his face was murderous. Without a pistol menacing his sister she knew there would have been a terrible fight. Within minutes, the cart had been swallowed up in the darkness.

"We make a fine pair, you and I," Francis said harshly, pulling Katherine into his arms. "But I swear if you ever look at a man again as you looked at Justin Douglas tonight, I'll whip you until you have no skin left on your body. Do you understand me?"

She nodded wordlessly, chilled by the threat. He was jealous of her love for Justin. She would never have believed him capable of such an emotion.

"I doubt if I shall ever look at any man again," she said tonelessly. Who else would look at her with Justin's dark eyes, hold her in arms that were both cruel and tender, kiss her until the ground moved beneath her feet?

"You will look at me, Katherine, and in time that love-mist in front of your eyes will vanish." As if to prove his words he tilted up her chin and thrust his mouth on hers. The unleashed passion in his kiss shocked Katherine to the very depths of her being. For a moment she was still, then in desperation she began to fight against the arms which enfolded her, but they only tightened until she was held immobile. "It's time I taught you I am not to be trifled with – not any more. I shall expect complete obedience from you as my wife."

She was aware of Sarah's horrified expression as she closed her eyes and submitted in silence to the kisses being pressed on her mouth and hair and throat – to the hands exploring her body. He was treating her like one of his loose women and it nauseated her, but for every minute she endured it, Justin was being taken further away from danger.

"Francis – please take me back to the house."

She had always fought him before . . . the complete lack of resistance in her now was arousing in him the desires he had been compelled to suppress on other occasions. She thought he meant to ignore her, then slowly she was released. In the moonlight she saw he was smiling and knew the reprieve had only been momentary.

"Why not? It was my intention to spend the night elsewhere and return early enough to discover the escape of the prisoner myself, but I have changed my mind. You got out without being seen – we will go back the same way and celebrate our – understanding. In the morning I will be able to provide you with a perfect alibi, will I not?"

"Mistress Katherine – no!" Sarah cowered back as he wheeled on her.

"You will go to your room, girl, and stay there until morning. If you breathe a word of what you have seen and heard tonight I'll have you put in the pillory for a week. Do I make myself clear?"

"Do as you are told," Katherine said gently. "In the morning everything will be as it should be." She had forgotten the existence of the guards until that moment. They would testify to her involvement in Barbara's escape, and in doing so free her from the promise she had given Francis.

As Katherine and Francis reached the steps, the trooper who

had been guarding Barbara's room and the sergeant came out of the house. One side of the latter's face was streaked with blood from the wound on his head where Simon had struck him.

"Captain Grahaeme – at least you have caught her." The sergeant lowered his musket at the sight of his superior officer. Katherine thought he looked angry enough to have used it on her. "Have the others got away – the girl – the Douglas brothers?"

"Others?" Francis looked down at Katherine and his fingers curled so tightly around her wrist that she winced in pain. "I saw no one else. Are you telling me the prisoner has escaped?"

"With her help." The trooper glared at Katherine. "She tricked me and I was knocked unconscious."

"I found him bound and gagged in the prisoner's room," the sergeant interrupted.

"What happened to your head, man?" Francis demanded, tight-lipped.

"One of the men attacked me."

"You saw Mistress Ashley with the prisoner?"

"She was telling them what to do. Without her help they could not have got out of the house."

Katherine began to smile . . . she could not help it. Even the mounting anger on Francis's face did not deter her. Justin was free and on his way to safety. At least she had given him some chance. . . .

"You knew!" She cried out as the agonizing pressure on her wrist increased. "You've played me for a fool once too often, Katherine. Now it's time to teach you a hard lesson, and it will begin with the execution of your lover which I shall have great pleasure in making you witness."

"It's too late – you will never catch him now," Katherine breathed jubilantly. "He's too clever for you. The King's Shadow is free, Francis – and I don't know where he has gone, so you cannot beat it out of me."

"You never intended to keep your word."

"I would have said anything – done anything – to gain his

life and his freedom." She laughed in his face and was abruptly flung backwards into the arms of the two soldiers.

She was still laughing as they dragged her upstairs and locked her in her rooms while Francis Grahaeme rampaged through the house like a wild animal. Laughter that echoed through the desolate emptiness of the rooms, mocking those who sought to destroy her and the man she loved. Wild, hysterical laughter which released days of pent-up emotion and stifled fears – until at last there was no more . . . and in its place came tears.

She lay on the bed where Justin had lain a short while before, her cheek resting on the pillow which still bore the imprint of his head and her fingers closed around the locket nestled in the warm hollow between her breasts. She was as close to him as if he was beside her in the darkness. It was something no one could take from her.

She was aroused from a deep sleep by the sound of loud, angry voices, the banging of doors and the heavy tread of boots on the stairs outside her room. As she lay trying to gather her scattered wits, the door was flung open and her father stormed into the room. He looked tired and dishevelled. His clothes were streaked with dirt and his face was red with anger. Behind him stood the sergeant, who scowled across at her, probably cursing her for his aching head.

"Where is she?" Nathaniel Ashley demanded bleakly.

Katherine sat up and regarded them both with a quizzical look.

"Who, father?"

"Damnation, girl, don't try my patience too far! Barbara Douglas, where is she?"

"Gone. Has no one told you?" She stood up, smoothing out the skirts of her creased dress. "Did you catch the King?"

The look directed at her by her father was surely meant to shrivel her to a pile of ashes, Katherine thought.

"We caught the men we were after. Neither one was Charles or knew where he was to be found," the Major returned. "Do you realize what you have done?"

"Yes. I have probably ruined your chances of promotion – Francis's too. What a pity!"

He stared at her as if she had taken leave of her senses.

"Francis has taken a troop of men and gone after your friends. You had best pray he brings them back. Betrayed by my own flesh and blood! It is unbelievable. Yet the proof is in your refusal to deny you had any part in this escape – or were forced to participate in it under threat of injury or death. You stand before me an unrepentant sinner – just like your mother. You realize I must inform Lord Cromwell of this immediately. I can no longer shield you."

"I have never asked it of you. As for shielding me, it was more to protect yourself, wasn't it? Now it has failed, you will denounce me as a traitor with tears in your eyes. I'm sure you will be very convincing, Father. Don't worry, I will see no blame is attached to you." Katherine's eyes blazed with a sudden show of emotion. "But I will never forgive you – as my mother did."

An hour after the first encounter with her father, he demanded her presence in the library and she left her room under the watchful eye of the sergeant.

She had been expecting such a summons and had spent the time she was alone mustering all her courage to endure what she suspected was to be a war of nerves. She had changed into a clean dress with a fresh white collar and cuffs, her hair had been carefully brushed back beneath a linen cap. The flash of surprise in her father's eyes told her he had not been expecting such a composed figure, and the slight victory gave her added courage. Francis was not present in the room. She wondered how much he had told her father before he left – if anything?

Nathaniel Ashley sat behind his huge desk in front of the french windows, and as she looked past him into the gardens she thought of the success of the previous night and regretted nothing. Dr Richardson sat in a high-backed chair a few feet away beside Sarah. She looked towards them with a slight inclination of her head, acknowledging their presence, but nothing more. She noticed her father was clearly disappointed she had not betrayed more emotion.

"Sit down, Katherine. You know why we are all gathered here, of course?"

She obeyed him, folding her hands loosely in her lap, forcing herself not to display any agitation.

"No, Father, why should I? You have doubtless been told of my part in Barbara's escape; what more do you want? Dr Richardson merely came here to bandage her wound, as any good doctor would do. And Sarah? She knew nothing of what I did. I did not want to involve her in such danger."

The scene was laid. She risked a quick glance at her two friends and saw they understood they were to confirm her statement. Poor Sarah's eyes were red from crying, she noticed, but a few tears and a few lies were better than years in prison.

"You obviously gave no thought to your own dangerous position. Tell me of your involvement with this King's Shadow. He was here last night, wasn't he?"

"Yes."

"He came to you because he knew you would help him?" the Major snapped. "What is he to you?"

"I love him." Katherine had decided that in some instances the truth could do no harm, and she did not hesitate with her answer. She heard Sarah draw in her breath sharply, but did not look at her. She had eyes only for her father and the ugly suspicion growing in his expression.

"So – you are his plaything."

"I said I love him. I did not say he feels the same way about me," Katherine answered, flushing acutely. "He does not."

"Yet you gave him shelter and helped him to free his sister?"

"As he helped me when one of your men used me as a target. He saved my life. What I did in return was a small thing."

"It seems there have been several small incidents, I recall. At the Douglas house, for instance, when you attempted to warn not only the entire family of traitors, but the fugitive Charles himself. You gave aid to Barbara Douglas and planned her escape. Did you also send word to her brothers and warn them she was here?"

"You did that when you leaked the news of my supposed

part in the attempted capture of the King. How could I send any messages? I have not been allowed to leave the house, and I would not entrust anything so important to anyone else."

"I believe that at least. You maid was under constant surveillance each time she went out." The man glanced at the middle-aged man busily writing beside him and then at Katherine, and she felt her heart lurch unsteadily as she realized the implication. Every word she uttered was being recorded. Her admitted love for Justin – the help she had given him – all proof of her guilt, perhaps to be given in evidence against her at a later date. She felt suddenly very cold and barely suppressed a shudder. This was the awakening into awful reality, and there was no turning back. She had always accepted it in her heart, now she was being forced to admit it openly and it was an alarming moment.

Nathaniel Ashley did not speak for some while, but continued to sift through the sheaf of papers before him. Katherine stared at her hands, suspecting he was deliberately prolonging her agony, and she prayed she would not weaken.

"I do not think I need detain you any longer, doctor. You came to tend the prisoner Douglas at my daughter's request and were not aware of her true intentions. Was the injury serious? I mean, serious enough to delay her from travelling?"

"Hardly – it was superficial, as I told your sergeant. The girl obviously panicked and tried to kill herself – or at least harm herself sufficiently to keep herself here until an escape could be arranged."

"Possible, but too drastic. She must have panicked, as you say. She was able to move then? My sergeant states he saw her in the library, apparently none the worse for her little escapade."

Dr Richardson deliberated the question for a moment, looking at the sergeant who stood behind Katherine's chair as he did so.

"I am sure your man is an able fellow when it comes to fighting, but where medicine is concerned I think you must agree I have the better qualifications," he replied slowly, adding in a harder tone: "I have never had my word doubted before, Major, and I would remind you I was invited into this house – I did not offer my services."

"No, you came at my daughter's request. Your point is taken. You may go. As for you . . . "

Katherine raised her head, but her father's attention was centred on Sarah, who began to look apprehensive under his close scrutiny. She heard the door close behind her and knew the doctor had departed. She was not sure if his story was altogether believed, but at least it could not be disproved, and that was the important thing. He would most certainly be watched, but he was a careful man and would expect surveillance of some kind. She had no cause to worry on his account.

"Come here, girl."

Sarah was near to tears as she approached the desk. Katherine guessed she was more frightened for herself than her mistress who was, after all, the Major's daughter. Even if he did not care for her, he would never allow her to be sent to prison – whereas she, Sarah, was only a servant girl and of no importance to anyone. He could do what he liked with her.

"I've done nothing wrong, sir – truly," she sniffed. Katherine stood up, ignoring the warning look directed at her, and slipped a comforting arm around her maid's shoulders.

"Then you are a good girl?" The Major reached for the Bible at his finger tips and drew it to him. "Do you attend church regularly?"

"Oh yes, sir. Mistress Katherine will tell you."

"She can tell you nothing, Father. Please leave her alone. Can't you see how frightened she is?" Katherine said with rising anger. How glad she was the sergeant had been knocked out before he could see Sarah! She could not be connected with the escape.

"She has nothing to fear if she is innocent. So you go to church every Sunday. And you love your mistress?"

"Indeed I do, sir."

"You would lie for her, of course?" Nathaniel Ashley leaned back in his chair, his arms folded across his chest, his hard eyes narrowed as Sarah turned and stared into Katherine's colourless face.

Katherine read his mind and knew that if she did not act quickly he would intimidate Sarah so completely she would confess to anything he asked of her.

"I have already told you Sarah knew nothing of my plans, Father. She was in her room when Justin and his brother broke into the house. It was I who distracted the guard outside Barbara's room – I took them out through this very room to where their horses waited by the stream. She did not even see them."

"I am not convinced of her guilt" – the Major's fingers toyed with the brass binding around the Bible – "nor of her innocence. She was not seen last night, but that does not mean she was not there."

"I swear she was not!" Katherine cried.

"Dare you?" Her father demanded, pushing the book in front of her. "As God is your witness, give me your most sacred oath that no one in this house aided you in your treacherous actions. If you lie, may you roast in the fires of the hereafter."

Katherine felt herself sway unsteadily. She put out a hand and steadied herself on the side of the desk – and then slowly placed her other hand down on the Holy Book. The words refused to come – she felt rising panic and then, in a voice so clear she could not believe it was her own, she said,

"I swear before God, I – and I alone – am responsible for the escape of Barbara Douglas. I was helped by no one in this house and I confided in no one. Are you satisfied, Father?"

Father and daughter faced each other – measured and challenged each other. With a brief nod, Nathaniel Ashley absolved Sarah, and the girl turned and wept in Katherine's arms, but the victory was a brief one. Sarah was ordered to find work in the kitchen and Katherine was returned to her room and locked in. Her meals were brought to her by the dour-faced housekeeper, whose contemptuous expression was more eloquent than words. Apart from that one person, she saw no one until her father came to visit her late that night. To her surprise he carried neither Bible nor cane, but several pieces of parchment. So she was not to be beaten this time, she thought, rising to her feet. He glanced down at the untouched tray of food on the table and then into her defiant features.

"I suggest you eat what is brought you. You may have need of your strength to face what lies ahead."

"And what is that?" Katherine asked, stiff-lipped.

Her father held out the documents. She saw that the ribbon around them bore his seal.

"Everything is here. From the moment you met Justin Douglas and conspired with him to aid the fugitive Charles, under the pretence of having him captured – to your part in the escape of Barbara Douglas from this house. This will be sent to Hampton Court. You are in God's hands."

"No, Father, I am in yours." Katherine turned away from him, beginning to feel very alone and frightened. "I know I can expect no mercy. I ask none."

"Have you no repentance in you?" the Major demanded. At this point he had obviously expected tears – some show of weakness at least, but she was as composed as when she stood before him in the library and condemned herself out of her own mouth.

"Why should I be sorry? I have done nothing wrong."

"You have been bewitched. That man and his licentious ways have turned your head. Dear heaven – now I understand! He has seduced you. Is that what happened, Katherine? He has shamed you, and you are too proud to tell me. Confess it to me now and I will tear up this document."

"Seduced me!" Katherine swung round on him, her cheeks flooding with scarlet. "How dare you presume such a thing?"

"Do not be ashamed. You were alone together and he no doubt exercised the great skill gained from all his affairs with painted court women to make you yield to him. It is understandable – you are so young and inexperienced – "

"Stop it, Father, you disgust me! I will not confess to such a monstrous lie, not even to make things easier for you, which is the only reason you want me to do it. If you send that letter to Cromwell I stand accused of treason. Me! The daughter of Nathaniel Ashley. People will stare at you in the streets, whisper behind your back and you won't like that, will you, Father? Your own men might even begin to wonder where your own loyalty lies. No – I will not say Justin Douglas seduced me, because he did not. He is a gentleman, not an animal. A soldier, not the cold-blooded murderer you wanted me to believe. In many ways you share the guilt of what I have done. You lied to me. If you had not done so I would never have involved myself with him in the first place, seeking revenge. Send your findings – they cannot hurt me. It is too late for that."

Her father's mouth twisted into a sneer. "So he scorned you, did he? Is that why you didn't go with him? Didn't your gallant cavalier want to be burdened with a common major's daughter? He has taken everything and left nothing, except the prospect – if you are lucky – of spending the rest of your life in some dark prison cell. Think on it, Katherine. I will not send the document until the morning."

"Send it. We have nothing more to say to each other," came Katherine's final answer.

CHAPTER TEN

FOUR days after Nathaniel Ashley had sent the damning proof of his daughter's guilt to the Lord Protector of England, Oliver Cromwell, Francis Grahacme returned to the house in Newbury. Katherine watched him ride into the courtyard from her bedroom window and was quick to notice a self-assurance she knew he should not have possessed under the circumstances. If the truth was ever known – and it had become apparent from her father's silence that he had no knowledge of what had really happened that night – he too could be arrested for aiding and abetting the escape of one of the most wanted men in the country. Francis looked up at the house as he entered, directly at her window, and she was dismayed to see him smiling.

Sarah was unusually quiet when she brought Katherine's breakfast tray and proceeded to make the bed while her mistress picked at the food.

"Major Grahaeme has returned," she said at length.

"I know. Where is he now?"

"With your father. He has come from Oliver Cromwell himself, mistress. If you could have heard the way he was talking – as if he was the master here. Why, it was he who told me I could come back and look after you."

"His new position has brought with it the power he has always wanted," Katherine said quietly. "Take the tray, Sarah, and come back later. I want to be alone."

"Mistress Katherine, you won't make him angry, will you?" The maid paused in the doorway, looking anxiously into her mistress's pale cheeks. It had been six days since the escape of Barbara Douglas and her brothers, and as many days since Katherine had been allowed out of her rooms.

"I doubt if it would matter any more. Don't worry about me, and do nothing yourself to antagonize either my father or Captain Grahaeme."

"It's Major Grahaeme now, mistress. He threatened me something terrible just before I came up here . . . I'll behave myself, you can be sure of that. He's devil enough to do all the awful things he said."

Katherine was surprised at the change in Sarah since Simon had departed, but could not find it in her heart to condemn her. Francis's threats had had the desired effect, however – she had been deprived of her last remaining ally.

She found it difficult to occupy her mind, and tried to concentrate her thoughts on the many memories of a happy childhood when her mother was alive, but the threat of what awaited her in London predominated. It was all the more ominous because she was not really sure what was to happen. She suspected she would be questioned by expert interrogators who would resort to other less pleasant means to loosen her tongue if she continued to refuse to co-operate. She had tried to convince herself her father would never stand by and allow her to be brought to trial on a charge as serious as treason, but on the occasions when he had visited her and she had looked into his hard face she had come to realize he would not lift a finger to help her unless she changed her story and confessed she had been seduced by Justin Douglas, who had then abandoned her to face the consequences alone. He assured her such a statement would lead to no more than a sharp reprimand from her judges and that his own good name would remain unsullied. She had deliberated on the suggestion for some while, realizing it was her only avenue of escape, but the whole idea was so repulsive to her that she knew she could never accept it.

Nathaniel Ashley came to her room later that morning and found her sitting in a chair beside the window, lost in her own thoughts.

"Have you come to your senses yet? Will you reconsider my suggestion while there is still time? Francis has returned from Hampton Court."

"Has he given up chasing the King's Shadow then?" Katherine asked coolly, and saw her father's brows draw together at the name.

"He has more important tasks now."

"Am I to be arrested then?"

"He has brought papers with him, but what they contain I know not. He is weary from his journey. No doubt he will show them to me when he has bathed and rested."

Francis's authority was showing itself already, Katherine thought, lowering her gaze. Her father spoke as if the younger man was indeed the master of the house.

"Well, girl, what is your answer?"

"You already have it." Katherine forced the words from between stiff lips. How easy it would be to accept his offer and be free from the uncertainty. One little word to assure her freedom, but in the same breath she would surely destroy the most important thing left to her – the purity of her love for Justin. Only she herself could destroy it and then she would have nothing. . . .

"You will not be able to retract your statement once you are in London. Be sensible, what good will it do you to continue this way? Whether you like it or not, I am the only one who can help you. I have no idea what passed between you and Francis, but he refuses to discuss that night with me. You have made a bad enemy there, Katherine, and for what? Your precious lover is undoubtedly in France by now and probably doesn't even remember what you look like. Men of his kind are never faithful to one woman. How this infatuation began I shall never know. From a good man like John Grahaeme into the arms of a womanizing cavalier!"

"Yes – John was a good man," Katherine replied slowly. "A far better man than I deserved. He was to have taken me away from you, Father. He knew that was my only reason for accepting his offer of marriage, but he was still willing to have me – that's how sweet and generous he was. I wanted to be free of you and the restrictions imposed on my life before I became like my mother."

"It was God's will she died. I am thankful she was brought

back to the right path before He saw fit to take her from me."

"Because she forgave you with her last breath? You will not find me so forgiving."

"And the love you have for this other man – this Douglas? What did he offer? A few moments of stolen pleasure – a silk gown that showed almost as much of you as the day you were born? Where was your escape with him? Perhaps he promised to take you to France . . . "

"Justin promised nothing. He gave nothing. He is in the service of the King, dedicated to his cause. No, I lie – he did give me something . . . an awareness of myself as a person. He taught me to look beyond my selfish existence and care for others, as he does. With Justin it is total commitment, something he inherited from his father. In understanding the way he is, I came to understand myself and to accept that no one will ever be as important to him as the King."

"You have said enough," her father broke in harshly, and stormed out of the room, slamming and locking the door behind him.

With a sigh Katherine turned to look out of the window again, totally resigned to whatever lay ahead. If the price of Justin's freedom was her own, then she was quite willing to pay in full.

No one came near her until the evening, and when the door was next unlocked she expected it to be Sarah with her supper. It was the maid, but without a tray.

"Mistress Katherine, he wants you to eat downstairs tonight."

"My father?" Katherine queried. The suggestion did not appeal to her.

"No, Major Grahaeme. In twenty minutes, he said."

"Did he now?" It was on the tip of her tongue to refuse, but what would be the use? She was no longer her own mistress. "Very well, tell him I will be down when I have changed. Sarah – is there any news? I saw you go out this afternoon. What are they saying in the town? Has – has the King been seen?" She could not bring herself to ask the most important question.

"I'm sure I don't know, mistress. I had no time to stop and gossip."

Katherine was appalled by the girl's lack of interest after all they had shared together. Could she have been so wrong about her character? An expression of disgust crossed her face and she turned away, and Sarah left her without giving her the words of comfort she so desperately needed. If only she knew Justin was safe. . . .

She washed and put on a clean dress and an embroidered linen cap over her braided hair and went down to supper, closely followed by one of the troopers who so diligently guarded her room day and night. The long table in the dining-room had been laid – in honour of Francis? she wondered, or – with a sudden chill of fear – as a kind gesture on the part of her father before he delivered some terrible news? Was she to be sent away in the morning – under arrest – disgraced? Her footsteps faltered and she stood in the doorway, pale and lacking the confident poise she had maintained until this moment.

Francis Grahaeme and her father were already seated. As soon as she joined them, the latter rose to his feet to give the customary blessing.

"Dear Lord, we thank Thee for the food Thou hast placed before us this night and humbly beg Thy blessing on all who sit at this table."

The words had never varied since she was a child. At every meal they were recited, day after day, year after year. Lifting her head, she looked across at Francis and found he was lounging back in his chair, watching her with an intentness that brought a flush of pink to her colourless cheeks. He looked pleased with himself and that unnerved her. Why, when one word from her in the wrong ear could wreck all his ambitious plans?

"I hope you are well," he said as Nathaniel Ashley sat down and the housekeeper began to serve them.

"Do you?"

"Your father tells me you still refuse to co-operate. No matter, I anticipated your stubbornness. You see how well I have grown to know you, Katherine. I learn well from past mistakes. I will not underestimate you again."

Katherine ate in silence, praying he did not guess how his words prolonged her anxiety, but knowing he did. He was playing with her, enjoying her agony of mind. She was glad when the simple meal was over and the two men rose. Quickly she said:

"Now you have reassured yourself I have not been spirited away, Francis, perhaps you will allow me to return to my room."

"Have you no interest in your future, Katherine?" he mocked, and she steeled herself for the worst.

"Do I have one?"

He came close to her, his piercing gaze sweeping her face. "You will be wise not to underestimate me either, my dear. Did you honestly believe I would allow your stupid infatuation for Douglas, or your father's incompetence in bringing you to heel, to spoil months of very careful planning?"

"You forget your manners," Nathaniel Ashley growled angrily.

"I forget nothing, old man. You are growing either soft or senile. If you had given Katherine to me in the first place instead of allowing my weak-kneed brother to lay claim to her, none of this would have happened. No association with Douglas . . . no slur cast on your name . . . no cloud over my head threatening my chances of getting everything I have ever wanted."

Katherine was unable to suppress a cry of amazement at his words. Her father's preference for Francis as a husband instead of John had been no secret, but she had not been aware Francis had ever seriously contemplated marrying her. So the odd embraces and stolen kisses had been more than just a game with him.

"You shouldn't be surprised, my dear – not at this late stage," Francis murmured. "I thought I had made my intentions quite clear."

"Intentions, yes. For a moment I thought you were about

to say feelings, but of course those are something you know little of."

The pale eyes watching her glittered with sardonic humour. "You will know the depth of my feelings for you soon enough. I admit in the beginning you amused me, Katherine. I enjoyed teasing you, making you angry, feeling the woman in you fighting against being released every time I kissed you. You suppressed that side of you well – soon I will change all that. As I have already told you, I expect complete obedience from my wife."

"Wife!" Nathaniel Ashley repeated harshly. "What talk is this? Katherine is to be sent to Hampton Court and then London – you said so yourself."

"You misquote my words. I said Katherine is to accompany me to Hampton Court – but as my wife, not as a prisoner."

"Are they not one and the same?" Katherine wanted to ask, but the words refused to come and she tottered backwards and slipped down onto the nearest chair, inwardly trembling. Was there not to be a trial after all – despite the papers her father had sent to Oliver Cromwell?

From inside his coat Francis produced several pieces of parchment and tossed them down onto the table. Nathaniel Ashley's face registered surprise, then puzzlement bordering on anger as he picked them up. Katherine recognized them immediately as the transcripts of her hearing. They still bore his seal – unbroken.

"How do these come to be in your hands? They were for the eyes of Lord Cromwell alone."

"Be thankful I intercepted them. I have saved your good name," Francis returned scathingly.

"To further your own ambitions," Katherine added dully. He had beaten her after all. Mixed emotions were confusing her mind. Relief at being suddenly free from the uncertainty of a trial and its outcome – despair at the realization he intended to keep her to her promise of marriage. Francis's wife! She looked into his face in silent anguish and watched a smile deepen the corners of the sensuous mouth. Soon he would be able to do more than just look at her. The thought of his love-making made her feel quite ill and she shivered, knowing the complete obedience he required would be gained in one of two ways – either by her complete submission without a fight or by brute force. So long as he achieved his aim he would not care which way it was, and she knew it was inevitable he must win in the end. It was not a pleasant thought.

Her father was still holding the transcripts and staring at Francis as if he was a stranger. It was the first time she could ever remember him being lost for words.

"If I understand you correctly, you intend to take Katherine from here and wed her?" he asked at length. "It is you who are growing soft. Have you forgotten what she has done? Who she gave herself to? One wrong word and you could end up beside her in prison. Have you considered that?"

"I have considered everything," came the confident reply. "Katherine will not be troublesome. By the time we reach Hampton Court I feel she will be well acquainted with my requirements. A house in London has been placed at my disposal. There will be entertaining to take care of and many other things to occupy her mind. She will have no time for memories – or foolish fancies. I shall see to that."

"You have forgotten Justin Douglas."

"If he is not in France by now he is probably lying dead in a field somewhere. My men found the cart the fugitives abandoned less than two miles from here and he could not have gone far on foot with that wound."

"Wound?" Katherine's father looked at her intently and then back at the younger man. "I have heard no mention of him being wounded before. Katherine – is this true?"

"Why should I have given you the advantage of such knowledge?" Katherine shrugged her shoulders. "Yes, he was hurt. He had to be carried out to the cart." She shut her mind to the thought of Justin lying cold and lifeless somewhere in the countryside. So long as she believed he was alive and safe, her own plight was bearable.

"Cart? You told me they had horses. To know any different would mean you were there too, Major Grahaeme. I demand an answer. Were you a witness to my daughter's activities that night?" Nathaniel Ashley snapped, in the old authoritative tones Katherine had grown to fear as a child. His thick brows drew together in a frown that was almost threatening, but neither the anger in his voice, nor in his expression, made any impression on Francis.

"It is of no consequence now," came the indifferent answer.

"He not only witnessed what I did, he helped me!" Katherine cried, jumping to her feet. "He let them all go in return for my promise of marriage."

"You allowed the Douglases to escort their sister from this house without lifting a hand to stop them?"

"Of what importance were they to me? A girl – a half-dead man and a boy. It was a calculated risk. Perhaps they would reach the coast, perhaps not. I had nothing to lose, but a great deal to gain. As Katherine once reminded me, Cromwell likes the men around him to have wives and families. He was well pleased when I told him who I was to marry. What do I care for the King, or his crowd of lace-clad clowns? They can go to the devil – or France – or the scaffold, I care not which, so long as they do not interfere with my chosen way of life. I think you had better sit down, old man, before you collapse. You still have one last duty to perform before Katherine leaves this house for ever."

"I will do nothing for you – or her."

"You will do exactly as I tell you. The sooner we are away from here, the sooner you can go back to your Bible. It is all you have left now."

"You will not escape retribution, either of you. God has witnessed all. . . ."

"I only worry about the living." Francis's tone hardened suddenly. "You will say nothing of what you have discovered tonight because you are too proud to admit your own flesh and blood betrayed you – as you were when you had the Douglas girl a prisoner here. You tried to make everyone believe Katherine had been your accomplice in the capture, and from the talk I have heard you were very successful. Pride is a sin, old man, a deadly sin, but it is one you will live with until the day you die. You kept quiet before – you will again. Everyone will believe you gave your blessing to our marriage because you will give the bride away, and afterwards you will give us a fine wedding breakfast before we leave for Hampton Court."

His words flowed over Katherine like a huge wave and left her dazed and reeling at the prospect of what her future was to be. He had left nothing to chance. She could see even her father was shocked. His pride had killed her mother, forced him to cover up her activities at the Douglas house with a pack of lies, and would continue to rule his life as always, thus eliminating the one stumbling block in Francis's path.

"When – when is this wedding to take place?" His answer gave her into the keeping of a man she feared and detested.

"I thought the day after tomorrow. I still have a few details to complete before my work here is finished, and Katherine will need time to make herself ready. You will, of course, return all the clothes and other items you removed from her room and provide whatever else she may require." It was an order, not a request. After a moment Nathaniel Ashley nodded and Katherine's last hope of a reprieve died within her. The day after tomorrow – so soon! But perhaps it was better that way. She did not want time to think – to remember. . . .

Crossing to her side, Francis tipped back her head to stare down into her blue eyes which were swimming with tears.

"Shed your tears. I want none of them when you are my wife. You will soon forget him – that I can promise you. Go to your room now – you have a great deal to do."

"Very well." Katherine did not argue, glad of the opportunity to escape from his loathsome company.

She was sitting in her rooms an hour later when the door opened and a trooper dragged in two heavy oak chests. She did not move from her chair, but stared at them in silence. Sarah pushed back the lids and began to pull out the contents.

"Isn't it wonderful, mistress? All your lovely things returned." She began piling the clothes onto the bed – stacking the books onto the floor to be sorted later. "I will have all your clothes pressed for you by morning, even if I have to stay up all night."

"The lamb being prepared for the slaughter," Katherine

murmured bitterly. Her eyes clouded with sudden pain as Sarah unpacked the trousseau she had made for her wedding to John, and her lips tightened into a determined line. Francis would never see her wear any of it. "Put that away," she snapped as her wedding gown came into view.

"But surely you will be wearing this?" The maid looked so surprised that Katherine wanted to hit her.

"Have you taken leave of your senses? Wear it to please Francis Grahaeme after the unhappiness he has brought into my life? I would rather tear it into a thousand pieces."

"How very foolish," a sardonic voice drawled from the doorway. Francis advanced into the room and stood for a moment looking down at the delicate creation. "A work of art, my dear – it would be a pity to waste it. You will wear it – to please me." It was a threat, not a request, and Katherine palcd slightly.

Bending down, Francis picked up the wedding gown and ran his fingers over the intricate embroidery Katherine had put around the simple neckline, and at that moment her self-control snapped. Jumping to her feet she grabbed at the cloth, intending to snatch it from his hands, but he held it fast. There was a sharp tearing sound, and before her eyes the bodice ripped in two.

"There – now you will never see me in it!" Katherine cried triumphantly.

A cruel smile masked the face of the man in front of her as he raised his hand and struck her with deliberate force across both cheeks. The blows rocked Katherine on her feet. She staggered back, both hands against the red marks his fingers had made.

"No – don't strike her again – please." She was aware of Sarah pushing in front of her – protectingly, she thought – until the maid began to speak in such a whining fashion that all Katherine's anger against her surged up again. "She won't be like this once you have taken her away to London. I'll look after her just as you wanted . . . I promise. It's his fault, you know – Sir Justin's – he turned her head, made her forget the true path. Please, Major, give her time . . . "

"She shall have time – between Newbury and Hampton Court," Francis returned coldly. "Stop pleading for her, girl."

Katherine's head was reeling, but she had heard enough to realize that Sarah had turned from a friend into an enemy. She was no longer her maid, but her jailer, under Francis's supervision.

"You are dismissed," she said as Sarah turned towards her.

"The girl takes her orders from me," Francis informed her. "You will find her your only ally if you continue to act in this fashion."

"Ally! Yours perhaps, but mine no more. I will not have her near me."

Francis shrugged his broad shoulders and indicated Sarah should leave them. Katherine was aware of the sudden pained expression on the girl's face as she hurried from the room, but it roused no compassion in her.

"Despite your objections she will accompany us to London," he told her. "As for your show of petty temper, I think a lesson is necessary to show you the error of your ways."

"You sound like my father, Francis. You will be quoting from the Bible next. Is this the new image for the Lord Protector? What is your lesson to be – a beating? I am quite used to that, you know."

"With you I think something more subtle is required. Tell me, what is it you fear most in this world? Not being deserted by Douglas or the likelihood of a trial which could have meant your death. Shall I venture a guess?"

"I am in no mood for your games." Katherine would have turned away from him, but he stepped forward and caught her by the arm, holding her fast. His smiling face was barely inches from hers.

"While one spark of hope still lives inside you, fear cannot enter. You are clinging to it now, as you have been ever since Douglas left this house. His wound was serious, Katherine, and they abandoned the cart not far from here. I wonder why? Do you know? Did they tell you where they were making for after all?"

"No." Katherine's heart was beginning to race unsteadily. What lay behind his words? "What are you saying?"

"While you think he still lives, you can hold onto memories – maybe even plan for the day when you might meet again. Would you like to see him again, Katherine?"

"Stop it! Why are you torturing me this way? I am going to marry you – isn't that enough?"

"No, it is not. I intend to make sure our days – and our nights – are not haunted by a ghost. Tomorrow I shall show you how to sever all links with the past. Good night, Katherine." He kissed her once on the mouth and left her, dazed and alone, to spend a sleepless night plagued by anxious thoughts.

She was awakened by the housekeeper early next morning, and sat up in bed to find riding clothes laid across a chair.

"What is the meaning of this? Where is Sarah?"

"I have no idea, mistress. I am only doing as Major Grahaeme told me. Breakfast is downstairs. He said you must eat before you go out."

"Out where?" Katherine demanded, but the woman had already left the room.

Her hands were trembling so much she could scarcely dress herself. Her nerves felt ragged and her eyes burned from lack of sleep. What secret knowledge did Francis have about Justin? And where were they going before eight o'clock in the morning? She ate alone in the dining-room. When she went outside two horses were saddled and waiting in the courtyard, and Francis stood beside them.

"Are we playing guessing games?" Her voice was not as steady as she would have liked, as she climbed onto one of the mounts.

"Patience, my dear. All your questions will soon be answered. Be grateful I am making it possible for you to start married life with a peaceful mind."

Katherine decided against asking further questions, knowing he was enjoying every moment of her discomfort.

"Have you sent Sarah away after all? She did not come to me this morning," she said at length. They were skirting the town and heading across open land. This was no simple morning ride, but she kept her fears well in check and tried not to think where their eventual destination might be.

"You upset the girl last night. She was obviously fonder of you than either of us realized. She has run away."

"But have you sent no one to look for her? When did she go? Why was I not told?" Katherine was appalled her anger had brought about such a situation.

"She has relatives at Donnington – no doubt she has run to them. Why do you care?"

"She was my friend once – before you bullied her into turning against me," Katherine replied bitterly. Poor Sarah . . . despite their differences, she prayed the girl would come to no harm.

They rode at a brisk pace and Katherine was constantly aware of Francis's close scrutiny. What was he expecting to see in her face? It was beyond her. And then the road suddenly became familiar; she had come this way with Justin. Ahead of them was the wood where she had been wounded. They were riding in the direction of the Douglas house. But why? Questioningly she looked at Francis's features, which betrayed no emotion.

"I see you remember where you are."

"Yes."

"Good. What are you thinking now, Katherine? Of him? Can you imagine he is riding beside you instead of me?"

"I have no recollection of what happened after I was shot," she answered through trembling lips. "All I remember is waking up in Justin's home." It was not the truth, but she would never share with Francis those treasured moments when Justin had nursed her through a night of fever, wrapped her in his cloak and cradled her close against his chest . . . touched his lips to her burning cheeks.

"How unfortunate." The inference was clear, but she chose to ignore it.

They paused on the hill overlooking the house, exactly as Justin had done. Gone was the white palatial mansion . . . in its place stood a gutted ruin. The whole of the top storey had been destroyed in the fire, only the lower ones remained, blackened, windowless, exposed to the elements. Through a mist of tears she saw her companion smile at the scene and start down the hill. Wishing she was a thousand miles away, Katherine followed.

She stared in silent regret at the flower gardens she had once walked in, now trodden down beneath the careless boots of the troopers who had tramped over them that night. What was Francis trying to prove? These memories were precious to her and would remain so through the years ahead. They could not be destroyed by bringing her to this spot again – instead, he had revived many more to comfort her aching heart. The arbour was in front of her, with the seat where she had sat with Justin. Beyond were the lodge and the lake. Her eyes clouded abruptly as Francis reined in and dismounted and then turned to help her down. They were on the edge of woods, at the place where Elizabeth Douglas had been shot down. The unmarked grave lay before her.

"Why have you brought me here?" Her voice was hardly audible. Another grave, freshly dug a few feet away, sent an uncontrollable shiver through her body. She snatched her hand from his grasp.

"To lay a ghost, my dear. His ghost. You can rest easy now you know where he is."

Katherine's eyes widened in horror. She reeled back against her horse, clinging to the saddle for support as her legs weakened with the shock.

"Are you saying ... " Her mind refused to accept the suggestion. "No, it can't be true. He was badly hurt ... but he isn't dead ... he isn't ... "

"Who else would be buried here? When the cart was found I suspected he had died and probably been taken home for burial, so I ordered my men to patrol this area and a thorough search revealed this. Ask yourself the same question I did. Knowing who was buried here – as most people do in these parts – who would profane her resting place by putting a common peasant near by? Who would risk capture to carry out what was perhaps a last request? Young Douglas, of course. He brought his brother here and buried him beside their mother before taking his sister to France."

"No!" Katherine moaned. Justin dead ... buried at her feet ... she would not, could not, believe it.

Francis reached out to catch hold of her as she turned and began to run, but she struck out at him blindly and darted past, along the path towards the house. He was an inhuman devil to torment her so vilely. He had destroyed the last vestige of hope in her, condemning her finally to reality and a marriage she had never before accepted within herself. When she thought of the house now, those two graves would rise up in her mind and the memory would bring pain ...

The house loomed up before her, gutted, desolate, the wind whistling eerily through the charred and broken beams. Part of the Great Hall was still standing and, at the far end of it, the fireplace which still kept its secret of the hidden passageway beyond. The thick, solid stones, although scorched, had survived the intense heat. Above the gaping chasm of the fireplace the Douglas coat-of-arms still clung proudly to the wall. The hawk in flight ... flying free. Justin was dead ... she was no longer free. She reached up and touched the cold stone, huge tears running down over her cheeks.

"Dear God, why could I not have been born a man?" she whispered brokenly.

"Enabling you to avenge the death of your lover perhaps?" Francis mocked from behind.

She wheeled on him, her lovely face contorted with grief and fury.

"Yes, I would kill you. For Justin – his mother – for all the poor souls you have killed or maimed or goaded for your own pleasures. You are an animal."

"Your spirit amazes me, dear Katherine. I look forward to our wedding night when I shall prove to you I am indeed a man."

She was caught up in his arms before she could move. The shock of the terrible blow he had delivered had drained her of all strength and her struggles soon ceased. She stood lifeless in his arms, uninterested, unaroused by the kisses pressed on her mouth. It would be bearable only if she pretended it was happening to someone else, but he had no intention of allowing her even that one small victory. His kisses grew more demanding, more passionate until her senses reeled and she cried out in pain:

"Francis – let me go . . . I beg you . . . "

"Yes, Major – let her go!"

That voice! She was dreaming. It came from behind them, from the direction of the fireplace. She was released so abruptly that she almost fell.

"Justin!" The joy in her voice brought an oath from Francis as he spun round, dragging at the pistol in his belt. His hand stayed on the butt as he looked into the two merciless faces confronting him and saw death mirrored there. Katherine found her voice again . . . stammered: "Justin – he – he said you were dead!"

He was a ghost, an apparition conjured up by her tortured mind; but then as the hard features turned towards her and broke into a smile she knew that by some miracle her prayers had been answered. Justin and Simon side by side, and behind them . . . Sarah!

"Oh, mistress, what has he done to you?" The sight of Katherine's distraught features brought the girl out of her hiding-place.

In her concern she passed too close to Francis, and in doing so gave him the chance he needed. Seizing her by the arm, he flung her with all his might at the two brothers. Katherine cried out as the three of them staggered back into the fireplace and Francis reached once more for his weapon. She threw herself forward onto his arm, so that the shot went wide; heard him cursing as he cuffed her on the side of the head, and she fell to the floor, the sound of a second shot ringing in her ears. And then strong hands were supporting her, cradling her head against a firm shoulder, and a voice she had never thought to hear again, except in her dreams, was saying:

"Kate – beloved. Open your eyes. Tell me you are not hurt."

Justin's anxious features swam before her hazy vision. She turned her face into his shirt, clutching at him with nerveless fingers. She felt his lips brush her cheek, the gentle caress of his fingers in her hair.

"I'm real, Kate. Don't turn from me, for the love of God. It's more than I can bear."

"He said you were dead and buried out there beside your mother. Oh, Justin, he wanted to destroy my love as he would have destroyed me once he had forced me into marriage."

"The grave belongs to my mother's favourite dog . . . it died in the fire. I buried it myself. Hush now, be still. I know all about your promise of marriage, thanks to little Sarah. She met Simon in the market last week and told him everything. Since then she's been feeding us with information. When you turned on her last night, she came here to us."

"Sarah, I'm sorry," Katherine whispered. How inadequate the words were to express her gratitude for all the risks the girl had taken. "Why did you not tell me? You knew I was almost out of my mind with worry."

"That was my fault," Justin interrupted. "I swore her to secrecy. After we had left you, Simon saw I was too weak to travel to the coast, so he brought me here and hid me in the secret tunnel with food and drink to last me until he could return. Then he arranged to get Barbara to friends of ours on the coast. She is safe, Kate, as we soon will be."

"Why did you stay so long when you knew the countryside was teeming with soldiers?" Katherine asked quietly.

"Because I love you."

She raised her head and stared at him disbelievingly. "Simon broke his word to me! Oh, Justin, don't give me pity . . . don't pretend to care for me out of gratitude, I couldn't bear that."

"Pity!" For a moment he looked so fierce that Katherine shrank back; then his face cleared and a smile touched the corners of his mouth – that mouth that was so dear to her she could not help reaching out to touch it with her fingertips. He caught them and held them there, a great tenderness in his eyes. "Love and hate are both violent emotions and so alike it's hard to tell where one ends and the other begins. I shall never know when I stopped hating and fell in love with you, Kate."

Masquerade

1. Masquerade have now published eight Historical Romances. Please tell us how much you have enjoyed any of those you have read:-

Title	Very much indeed	Very much	Not much	Not read it
The Runaways				
A Rose For Danger				
Eleanor and The Marquis				
The Secret of Val Verde				
The King's Shadow				
The Fortune-Hunter				
Puritan Wife				
Francesca				

2. Please tell us which of the Historical Romances you have read has, in your opinion, the most attractive cover:-

....

3a) Please tell us which historical periods you like best by ticking in the appropriate boxes

☐ Mediaeval ☐ Elizabethan ☐ Regency ☐ Victorian ☐ Other

b) If you have any favourite Historical Romance authors please give their names

....

4. Do you buy the monthly Mills & Boon Romances?

☐ Regularly ☐ Occasionally ☐ Rarely ☐ Never

Your name ....

Address ....

.... Post Code ....

THANK YOU FOR YOUR HELP

H.10/77 CN

Postage
will be
paid by
Mills & Boon
Limited

Do not affix Postage Stamps if posted in
Gt. Britain, Channel Islands or N. Ireland

2

BUSINESS REPLY SERVICE
Licence No. CN81

MILLS & BOON READER SERVICE
P.O. BOX 236
14 SANDERSTEAD ROAD
SOUTH CROYDON
SURREY CR2 9PU

"Now you are stronger you could have escaped without trouble, yet you stayed for me. That's madness." Katherine breathed.

"Love is something I managed to avoid – at least the entanglement love seems to bring with it, but now it looks as if I must face up to the fact I have found the woman I want for my wife. Love kept me here, Kate, a love so deep, so earth-shattering, I'm still trying to recover from the jolt it's given me. But it's here, inside me, and nothing in this world will ever move it. Say you believe me, Kate. Come with me – share my life and the little I have to offer."

"Francis," Katherine murmured weakly. He would stop them somehow, she had no doubt of that.

Justin moved aside slightly, allowing her to see for the first time the prostrate figure of Francis Grahaeme outstretched on the dusty floor behind them.

"I had to shoot him," Simon said quietly. "He would have killed us all if I had given him the chance . . . as he killed my mother."

Katherine nodded. She was unable to feel remorse at his death, knowing he would have afforded her none under the same circumstances.

Justin stood up and helped her to her feet. She held tightly to his arm, and the feel of the solid muscle beneath her hand told her this was no dream. She wanted to laugh and cry at the same time, so great was her happiness. Justin loved her! Wanted her for his wife!

"Are – are we to go to France?" she ventured to ask.

"Yes, where we will live in safety until I can come home and bring with me the new mistress of my home. We will be wed in France and Charles will dance at our wedding feast. We have a hard ride ahead of us, but the ship is all arranged, and Sarah has stolen clothes and horses. You will have an escort of two Roundheads to the coast, my love." His eyes grew suddenly serious as if he was contemplating the years ahead. "Do you realize how little I have to offer?"

"It is more than I have ever had in my life before," Katherine murmured gently. "We have each other. Our love will remain as true as that which your parents shared. I have only one fear. Oh, Justin, how will you bear exile? Will it make you bitter?"

"Don't fret, Kate, I am resolved to it so long as you are with me, and I know the time will come when the King's Shadow will return home to rebuild from the ruins we leave behind. My love – my own sweet Kate." Justin's arms enfolded her and she gave herself up to the ecstasy of his kisses. They were so engrossed with each other that it was several minutes before Simon dared approach to remind them they were not yet safe, and then discreetly went off to change into one of the Roundhead uniforms Sarah had stolen from the house before she left.

It was then, as they followed, that Justin told Katherine of the long days hidden in the secret passage, fever-ridden, tortured by his own thoughts when Simon returned to tell him of Katherine's great sacrifice, of his determination to set her free and get them all to safety in France – and a new life.

It would be a story to tell their children, he murmured, and she nodded, happy in the knowledge that day would now most certainly come....

CHAPTER ELEVEN

As a shadow fell across the sun-drenched pew where she sat in silent meditation, Katherine looked up expectantly, and a soft gasp escaped her lips at the sight of the Roundhead officer towering over her. She had been sitting for almost half an hour in the tiny chapel which lay beyond the secret passageway under the ruins of the Douglas house and had been so lost in her own deep thoughts she had not heard the wooden altar, which so effectively concealed the entrance, pushed to one side, or seen the tall, uniformed figure who emerged and stood watching her for a while before approaching.

"Justin! You frightened me almost to death." Her momentary panic vanished as she realized she was face to face with the man she loved and not one of her father's men come to snatch her back to a world she loathed and feared.

"Poor Kate. I'm sorry. Did you think Francis Grahaeme had come back from the dead?"

Katherine shivered at the name of the man who lay dead on the dusty floor of the Great Hall. He was dead, but it would be a long time before she could forget the harm he had done her. In the quiet solitude of the chapel, she had been trying to make plans for her future with Justin in France, but it was not easy. So much had happened to her since she had last been beneath his roof: the murder of his mother, Barbara's arrest, her own life threatened by a trial and possible imprisonment, Francis's attempt to force her into marriage in the hope of silencing the tongue which could disgrace him and wreck all his ambitious aims. She could not believe she was free of him as well as of her tyrannical father and all the dangers which had surrounded her for so many weeks.

"Kate, what is it, my love?" With a concerned expression,

Justin went down on one knee beside her, caught both her hands in his and held them tightly against his chest. "What thoughts are troubling you now?"

"I'm afraid."

"Of what, sweetheart? Your reaction to my appearance just now told me I shall pass as a Roundhead, and I have taken Francis Grahaeme's dispatches. If we are stopped, I have a letter from Cromwell himself instructing me to bring my future wife to London."

"And if the men who stop you knew Francis?"

Justin frowned at her. "What's happened to the spirit you showed less than an hour ago, Kate? Did it die with Major Grahaeme?"

"Don't be cruel, Justin. Can't you understand my fears? I thought I had lost you once; I was resigned to life, such as it would have been without you, and now, suddenly, you are here with me again, offering me all I ever dreamed about. I couldn't bear losing you again. If we were caught, you would be killed . . . I couldn't bear it . . . "

With an oath Justin gathered her against him, gently stroking her hair, pressing his mouth to her trembling lips, until he felt her begin to respond.

"Now listen to me." Gently he held her away from him, his eyes searching her colourless face. "Nothing will ever part us again. I swear it. We are in God's house, Kate. Before Him and you, I make that most sacred promise. Nothing will ever part us or harm the love I have for you. If there was a priest here I would marry you this instant. God only knows I have little enough to give you, only the proud name I bear and an undying love, but I give them both willingly. Tell me nothing has changed between us."

The anguish in his eyes brought a soft cry to Katherine's lips and she took his face in her hands and kissed him tenderly.

"Forgive me . . . I did not mean to hurt you, but I am so afraid to hope again."

"But you still love me?"

"More than my life. As long as we are together . . . "

"Then trust me. Francis Grahaeme is part of the past, along

with your father and everything unpleasant that has happened to you. Forget and think only of us, our life, the home we will make in France until we can return here and rebuild this place to give our children their rightful heritage."

"We will come back, won't we?" Katherine breathed. "We must. I want this to be my home, Justin . . . to share it with you and be as happy as your parents were . . . to watch our son playing by the lake – "

She broke off as Justin gave an amused chuckle. "So I am to have a son, am I?"

"A son first and then a daughter and after that . . . " Katherine's face began to regain some of its colour as she spoke, and he smiled in satisfaction.

"You see how easy it is to put the past out of your mind."

"Thank you, Justin, you did know how I felt. Shall we wait until dusk before we leave?" Suddenly she was anxious to be on her way, on the road which would take her to another country and another life.

"I would like to, but time is precious. We must risk daylight. Both Simon and I know these parts well; we should have no difficulty eluding any patrols."

"Where are we making for?"

"Shoreham. There is an inn on the coast, run by an old sea-captain friend of mine who still has dubious connections. The King and Barbara were smuggled onto one of his ships, as we will be when it returns from France, probably laden down with good old French brandy."

"Is he a smuggler as well as an inn-keeper?" Katherine asked in surprise.

"In his time Jonas has been many things, none of which matter to me, Kate. He has the means for our escape and he is loyal. That is what counts. Simon is waiting with the horses. Are you ready now?"

Katherine stood up and took a last, lingering look round the tiny chapel, and then gave a slight nod.

"Yes, Justin. I am quite ready."

It had begun to rain while Simon and Justin had been changing into their disguise as Roundhead soldiers. When they all emerged from the chapel and crossed the clearing into the trees where the horses waited, black clouds above them threatened a heavy deluge, and they had ridden less than five miles before a thunderstorm unleashed its fury on them. Katherine wore only her riding habit, which was soaked within minutes. Her loose hair clung to her face, blinding her as she rode. Justin, riding slightly ahead with Simon, swung his horse about and came back, motioning to some trees ahead which would give them some sanctuary until the storm passed. For almost an hour they sheltered from the downpour, huddling miserably together for warmth. At last Katherine could stand the waiting no longer.

"We must go on, Justin."

"Katherine, you are soaked to the skin – you need dry clothes."

"You said time is precious. The longer we remain here, the greater the risk of our being caught. Francis will soon be missed from the house, or someone could have discovered those uniforms are missing. You know I am right. We *must* go on."

Justin nodded, wiping the rain from his eyes. He smiled as he reached out and smoothed her wet hair away from her determined face.

"I hope Jonas's cellars are well stocked with brandy – we shall all have need of it by the time we arrive."

"How – how far have we to go?" Katherine asked, a slight tremor in her voice.

"We must avoid the coast road until the last possible moment," Justin returned. "Forty miles, perhaps a little more. If we ride hard we shall all have dry clothes and a bed to sleep in by nightfall."

The rain continued to hamper their progress throughout the day. Simon's horse stumbled on muddy ground and they all had to walk for an hour until the animal could take his weight once more. Justin stayed close to Katherine as the day wore on, as if he sensed that her strength was gone and only sheer determination kept her in the saddle. She was wet and cold and reeling with the strain imposed on her by the tormenting ride, but she shut her mind against her aching head and back and the cramp which was tying her left leg into agonizing knots. It was late afternoon, she told herself . . . only another few hours at the most. She saw nothing of the countryside through which they passed, as on another occasion when she had ridden with Justin. But then she had been cradled in his arms. How she longed again for his strength to give her courage, for hers was gone. It was dark. Were they lost? Her eyes closed with sheer tiredness as Justin ordered them to walk their horses for a while, and she began to sway in the saddle. His hand was suddenly on her arm, steadying her, and the relieved note in his voice in her ear brought her back to her senses.

"Kate, look down. In the curve of the bay . . . "

They were riding on the cliffs overlooking the sea. She could hear the pounding of the waves far below her as her weary eyes searched the darkness and saw, at last, the friendly lights of their destination.

The inn which had hidden the King of England for almost a week was owned by one Jonas Rigg, who had accumulated a small fortune sailing the high seas. Retirement had brought with it a wife and another profitable business. Two fast ships, manned by able captains and well-paid crews, ensured his cellars were always well stocked, and a little of the excitement of the old life remained to alleviate the boredom of respectability.

Katherine was aware of a giant of a man coming out into the courtyard to greet them as they rode in. Despite his age, which must have been about fifty, he still retained a head of flaming red hair and a beard to match. No sooner had Justin dismounted than he was seized in a fierce hug and slapped soundly on the back.

"My boy, you're here at last. So you've brought company then? Simon said you might. Who's this bedraggled wench, then?" He was looking at Sarah as he spoke. The maid gave a squeal of indignation and moved closer to Simon as if expecting to be menaced by a cutlass at any moment.

"Her name is Sarah and she's Simon's responsibility. The

lad has the notion he should be settling down," Justin returned, a smile lighting up his tired features.

"And you, boy. I've heard tell you have the same idea."

"It comes to us all in the end, Jonas, even to you." Justin turned to Katherine and held out his arms, and she almost fell out of the saddle into them. Her legs felt as if they were no longer part of her and Jonas Rigg uttered an oath as she swayed and clutched at Justin's jacket.

"Introductions can come later, Justin, the poor child is exhausted. Bring her inside to the fire and I'll tell Meg to make hot drinks for everyone."

Katherine felt Justin lift her and then knew no more until she recovered from her faint and found herself wrapped in a blanket in a large chair before a blazing fire. Justin was bending over her trying to force some brandy between her lips, and Simon and Sarah hovered anxiously in the background. She felt foolish for allowing herself to give way to her relief and tried to sit up, but Justin pressed her gently back.

"Lie still, Kate. Jonas's wife is preparing a room. I will take you upstairs in a moment when you are warmer."

"The ship – is – is it here?" Katherine stammered, suddenly afraid the nightmare journey had been for nothing. What if they were stranded?

"It will be. Some time tonight," Jonas broke in, bending over her chair. "Don't you worry your pretty little head about a thing. What you need most is sleep. Take her up, Justin, and then we can talk."

"He's right, Kate." Justin ignored Katherine's protest and lifted her out of the chair. Sarah hurried ahead of them up the winding stairs to the room where a rosy-cheeked woman was turning back the covers of a large and very comfortable looking bed. "Here she is, Meg. Put her to bed and refuse to listen to any arguments. Sarah, stay with her if necessary."

"No, she will catch her death of cold if she doesn't change into dry clothes," Katherine protested. "I promise I will go straight to bed, Justin."

"See that you do." He bent over her and, gently taking her face in his hands, kissed her lingeringly on the mouth, disregarding the other two women in the room. "Go to sleep and dream of tomorrow, Kate. Good night, my love."

In a borrowed nightgown two sizes too large for her, Katherine lay drowsing in the large bed. The open window allowed the sound of the sea to invade the room. Somehow she found it a comforting sound. The first signs of feverishness she had experienced upon reaching the inn had vanished, and she lay warm and comfortable beneath the heavy covers, all her previous fears forgotten. Nothing could touch them now. Tomorrow she would sail away to a new life in France with Justin and soon she would be his wife . . .

"Katherine! Are you awake?"

That voice! Katherine sat up, startled. Barbara Douglas was peering tentatively around the bedroom door.

"You – you are supposed to be in France!" she said weakly.

"Don't you lecture me too," Barbara replied with a grimace. She slipped into the room and closed the door behind her. Katherine held out her arms and embraced her warmly. "I have just spent several minutes with Justin which he made most uncomfortable for me because I am still here."

"He told me you had gone to France with the King."

"That was his idea, not mine. I persuaded Simon to let me stay here and wait for you both. How could I go away, Katherine, not knowing if Justin was alive or dead, or if anything had happened to you? Oh, it is good to see you again, and with my brother too. Have you settled things between you?"

Katherine nodded, her cheeks faintly blushing under the other girl's scrutiny.

"I am to be his wife, Barbara. You don't know how happy I am at this moment."

"Happy, but very tired. I must let you get some rest, or Justin will never forgive me. He gave me strict instructions not to disturb you, but I just had to see you again."

"You always were an uncontrollable little minx," Justin drawled from the open doorway, and Barbara leapt off the bed as if it had suddenly become red hot. "Don't look so worried, I am grateful for your concern over Kate, but you've kept her from her rest long enough. Off to bed with you now – we have an early start in the morning."

As Barbara slipped obediently out of the room, Justin closed the door behind her and came across to the bed. He was smiling, as from behind his back he produced a decanter of brandy and a single glass. Katherine watched him with puzzled eyes as he sat on the edge of the bed, his dark eyes dancing with wicked lights, and filled the glass to the brim.

"What are we celebrating?" she asked as he held it out to her.

"This excellent brandy comes from the *Nemesis*, the ship now anchored out in the bay, Kate. It's French brandy."

Her eyes widened as she understood the implication of his words. "It has come?"

"And we sail on the first tide in the morning. Drink up, my love, with Jonas's blessings – and mine."

Katherine could only manage one mouthful of the strong brandy, and handed back the glass with the feeling that her cheeks were already glowing. Justin downed the remainder in one gulp and nodded in appreciation.

"At least France has something to offer me."

"Don't, Justin."

"Hush, Kate, don't reprove me. This is my last night in a land I have fought for most of my life . . . I am losing something very dear to me, so you will have to excuse the fact that I am now about to get very drunk with Simon and Jonas on board the *Nemesis*."

"Can I not take the place of what you are about to lose?" Katherine asked quietly.

Justin reached out and almost reverently touched the locket suspended about her neck.

"You are part of me as I am part of you, but I am leaving so much behind, Kate . . . I am being torn in two."

His cry touched her heart. She slipped her arms about his neck and drew his face down to hers, kissing him as she had never kissed him ever before. Then, with a tremulous little laugh, she pushed him away.

"Go and get drunk then. Tomorrow let both of us leave the past behind."

Katherine awoke to a dull, grey morning. It was drizzling with rain and a thick mist obscured the bay and the ship at anchor beyond the rocky point, but she was not disheartened. It would mean they could slip out to sea undetected, she thought, and quickly dressed herself, eager to rejoin Justin and begin the last lap of their journey.

As she came downstairs the delicious aroma of freshly baked bread invaded her nostrils and led her directly to the kitchen where Jonas's wife was bustling about. At the sight of Katherine she quickly wiped her hands on her apron and inquired what she would like for breakfast.

"I am not very hungry, Mistress Rigg," Katherine confessed. "Perhaps a little later when the others are up."

"You'll not see those two fine gentlemen of yours until mid-morning at least," Meg Rigg returned with a broad smile. "I've just sent provisions out to the ship and the man who came for them told me neither Sir Justin nor his brother is stirring yet. As for that husband of mine . . . "

"Are they that bad?"

"It does a man good to get drunk once in a while. Don't look so worried, child, that man of yours has a good head on his shoulders. I hear he outlasted everyone else. At the moment both he and his brother are safely tucked up below decks, waiting for you to join them. If you don't want to eat anything now I will give you something to take with you for later. Your maid has already gone aboard . . . I think she was a little concerned over Sir Justin's young brother."

"You are very kind, Mistress Rigg. I want to thank you for all the help you have given us. Neither Sir Justin nor I will ever forget you and your husband."

"Bless you for such sweet words, child. I'm honoured to have been able to help such a gentleman as Sir Justin and a lady like yourself. It does my heart good to see two young people so much in love. And to have had the King beneath my roof . . . It will be something to remember with pride for the rest of my days. Sit down now while I prepare some food for the trip."

"Is Mistress Barbara awake yet?"

"Not when I last looked in on her some fifteen minutes ago."

"I think I had better wake her," Katherine said. "I am anxious to go on board."

"That's only natural. Her room is at the far end of the landing – you can't miss it."

Katherine found the room and poked her head round the door. All she could see was the top of Barbara's head beneath the covers. With a smile she sat on the edge of the bed and gently but firmly shook her into wakefulness.

"Come on, sleepyhead, it's time to be leaving. Everyone is waiting for us."

"I'm still tired." The other girl blinked up at her sleepily.

"You can sleep on the ship. Do hurry." Katherine found Barbara's clothes and stood by impatiently as the girl dressed herself. From the window she could see the *Nemesis* at anchor, hear the sounds of great activity on board as preparations were made to set sail – and with mounting excitement saw a small rowing boat leave the ship and head towards dry land.

"I think someone is coming to collect us," she said, turning to Barbara, and the other girl smiled as she saw the happiness mirrored in her eyes.

"Justin, of course."

"I very much doubt that. Mistress Rigg told me both Justin and Simon did rather a lot of celebrating last night. Sarah has gone ahead to minister to them until we arrive."

"I have forgotten the last time Justin was able to relax with friends and not be afraid for his life – or ours. Well, I am ready now. Shall we go down . . ."

Her voice trailed off into an empty silence. Katherine turned from the window where she had been watching the approach of the rowing boat, and at the sight of the man standing in the doorway before her she grew deathly pale and instinctively stepped back, her lips silently forming his name. It was not possible – he was dead! She had left him lying face down in the dust at the Douglas house after Simon had shot him. Her horrified gaze took in the ugly twist to his mouth, the dried blood which matted the hair above one temple, the pistol levelled in her direction. He swayed slightly as he came into the room, and kicked the door closed behind him, but the hand holding the weapon was steady.

"No, Katherine, I'm not a ghost. Be still, both of you. I shall shoot the first one who moves," Francis Grahaeme said coldly.

Barbara cast a desperate glance over her shoulder at her friend. Katherine shook her head, indicating she should do exactly as she was told.

"I don't think you would be foolish enough to fire that here and bring half a dozen men rushing to our aid," she said defiantly.

"The woman downstairs has told me everything I want to know, including the fact you are the only ones here. Oh yes . . . and I have seen the sailor coming ashore. He will prove most useful."

"What have you done to Mistress Rigg?" Katherine cried. She could not believe the woman would willingly have given the information Francis demanded.

"I suggest you save the concern for yourself. Believe me to be in deadly earnest when I say I will kill you if you don't do exactly as I say." He paused, his eyes narrowing as her expression became even more defiant. They had matched wills before and she had won then. "You have shown you have little regard for your own life, my dear, but I suspect Mistress Douglas will not have your capacity for self-sacrifice."

"What do you mean? What are you going to do with me?" Barbara's hands flew to her mouth. Even Katherine felt a sudden chill of fear run through her. She was prepared to risk her own life as she had once before, but not that of Justin's sister.

"Francis, let her go. I'll do anything you want, even go away with you this very moment – we will be married as you planned."

The smile on Francis Grahaeme's face was ugly as he stared into her ashen features.

"Yes, you will marry me, Katherine. That much has not

changed – will not change, whatever you do. Mistress Douglas, tie Katherine's hands behind her back; tear strips from your petticoats. Don't stand there gaping at me, girl, or I shall do it for you. Katherine will tell you I do not have the manners of a fine gentleman where women are concerned. That's right . . . tie them tight. Now gag her."

With a sinking heart Katherine submitted to being bound and gagged. She did not know what Francis had in mind, only that it was useless to put up a fight. He would kill them both without hesitation if she did.

Backing to the door, Francis opened it and listened for a moment.

"Good, our visitor has arrived. Katherine, come and stand beside me." He pushed her against the wall beside the door and held the muzzle of his pistol against her temple. "Mistress Douglas, go downstairs and tell the sailor Katherine has been taken ill and Justin Douglas must return to the inn at once."

"You will kill him!" Barbara breathed. "No, I won't do it!"

"I don't want him dead . . . others will take care of that for me. If you refuse I will kill Katherine first and then you. I want him alive, girl, to watch the spectacle of his execution. I want him to sit in a dirty, stinking cell knowing Katherine is my wife and in my bed. Who knows, perhaps his judges will be lenient and merely imprison him for life? At least he would be alive – and so would you."

Katherine shook her head desperately. Not for one moment did she believe Francis would allow Justin to reach London, to speak of his own treachery in withholding information from Oliver Cromwell himself, but Barbara nodded, seizing at the bait he dangled before her. A faint hope was better than none at all.

"Be convincing," Francis warned as she went out onto the landing, "and stay at the top of the stairs where I can see and hear you."

Holding Katherine firmly by the arm, he forced her along the passage after Barbara, halting her several feet away as Barbara leaned over the balustrade and began to speak to the sailor who had just come in.

"Have you come to fetch us?"

"Aye, mistress. Are you ready?"

"I cannot come, my friend is ill. You must go back to the ship and tell my brother Justin that he is needed. Katherine is asking for him. Please, go quickly . . . "

She turned away, trembling visibly, and walked slowly back to the bedroom, ahead of Francis and Katherine. Pushing both girls to one side, he peered out of the window, giving a chuckle of satisfaction as he watched the boat put to sea again.

"Your acting ability is excelled only by your stupidity," he drawled, wheeling on them.

Katherine felt herself grow sick with fear. She made incoherent mumbling noises behind the gag and Francis reached across and pulled it away from her mouth.

"Speak up, my dear. Let me hear you beg for his life . . . there is very little time."

"You promised me . . . " Barbara cried. "You inhuman devil . . . you lied and I have helped you. What am I to do?"

"There is nothing to be done. I shall kill your brother, mistress, and then, when help arrives, I shall go out to the ship and bring in the last of the Douglas family of traitors. You will both be taken to London to stand trial."

"Help?" Katherine echoed faintly. Was there nothing he had left to chance?

"It suited my purpose to come alone, but did you really think I was foolish enough not to have taken precautions? Within a very short time at least two dozen troopers will be here. By then, of course, Justin Douglas will be dead. When I discovered him hiding here, he attempted to escape and I killed him. Who will believe either of you if you tell a different story? The sister of the dead man, herself a Royalist, and a self-confessed traitress who aided the King in his escape. Yes, Katherine, I lied to you too. Marry you now! And risk the possibility of your speaking up against me at some future date? No, I have other plans for you, my dear."

"Do you intend to kill me too on the journey and say again it was an attempted escape?" Katherine faltered. "It is the only way you will silence me, Francis. I will tell them everything, do you hear? Everything. They will know you for what you are – a liar, a bully, a murderer . . . "

"You may say what you wish, but I doubt if anyone will take you seriously. I still have the transcripts of your hearing, Katherine. Of course I shall have explaining to do as to why I did not hand them over straightaway, but I'm sure I can convince Oliver Cromwell I was concerned for your father's good name. He will back me up, as I am sure you are aware, and it will count in my favour that I not only captured two members of England's most disloyal house and killed the head of it, but that I put my own personal feelings aside and did my duty as a soldier, despite the grief caused by handing the woman I love over to the authorities for trial. I shall escort you personally, Katherine, just the two of us. You have plagued my life for many years . . . it is time I rid myself of this infatuation for you. Exorcised the devil, shall we say. By the time we reach London, you will be glad of the sanctuary a prison cell offers you."

Katherine leaned weakly back against the wall, trying to close her mind against the degradation he intended to force her to endure. Barbara gave a choked cry and hurled herself at him, incensed by the thought of her friend being used so despicably. With an oath Francis pushed her away from him, stepped after her, saying cruelly:

"You are of no further use to me." And with those words he brought the butt of his pistol down across her head. She fell face down across the bed and lay still.

"Let me go to her . . . " Katherine struggled against the hands which held her back against the wall. "You – you haven't killed her? Oh, for the love of God, Francis . . . "

"Be quiet!" He slapped her hard on one cheek, and the blow rocked her on her feet. Bright tears flooded her eyes. Barbara lay so still, her face obscured by her loose hair. There was no way of telling if she was alive or dead.

Francis glanced out of the window and she saw a sneer twist his mouth.

"The fly is about to enter the spider's web," he muttered. "You and I must be there to greet him, Katherine."

"Untie me, please," Katherine entreated. "Let me help Barbara."

She was ignored and hustled out of the room. With her

hands still bound behind her back, it was impossible to break free of his grasp.

"Where are we going?"

"Down to the beach."

As they passed through the kitchen, Katherine glimpsed the inert figure of Meg Rigg, sprawled in a heap beside the window, loaves of fresh-baked bread scattered around her.

"She hit her head as she fell," Francis said callously.

Katherine choked back a sob. First Justin's mother, now Meg Rigg, both helpless women.

"How proud you must be!" she said between clenched teeth.

Francis did not answer, but the fingers curled round her arm tightened until she had to bite her lip to hold back a cry of pain. It told her he was not immune to her taunts.

At the far end of the well-stocked cellars was a door leading to a passage which stretched out under the cliffs to the beach. The uneven floor they walked on was very narrow, barely wide enough for two people to walk side by side. The sound of the sea grew closer and with every step the terrible despair in Katherine's heart mounted. She could do nothing against Francis, nothing to help Justin except to shout a warning the moment she saw him – a warning she knew would not make him turn back. He would try to help her. Whatever she did, Francis had won the final round.

She stumbled as they came out of the dim tunnel into bright sunshine, grazing one arm against the rocks. Francis hauled her unceremoniously to her feet and pushed her on, heedless of the spots of red blood on the sleeve of her blouse. Katherine's gaze swept the sandy beach. It was empty, but her relief was short-lived as she saw the boat putting out from the *Nemesis*. Justin had received her message. Francis followed her gaze and she saw him smile in satisfaction.

"How gallant," he sneered. His eyes were on her face as he took out his pistol and reloaded it.

"I won't shoot him until he has seen you, Katherine. He shall have one last look at you and you at him."

"Have you no heart . . . no conscience?" Katherine began to sob quietly. She had tried desperately to keep the tears in check, but the helplessness of her situation overwhelmed her. Her tears would amuse him, but she was past caring.

The boat altered course slightly and came towards them. With all her might Katherine flung herself against Francis, while his hands were still occupied with the pistol. He swore as she caught him off balance and he fell backwards onto the sand. She almost lost her own balance, but recovered and began to run towards the water's edge, screaming at the top of her voice.

"Justin . . . it's a trick . . . go back!"

Her voice echoed along the deserted beach. She glanced back over her shoulder to find Francis was coming after her, not running, as she was, but walking slowly, purposefully, confidently towards the water and the boat almost upon her. Katherine's strength gave out and she sank down onto the sand, choking for breath.

Strong arms were suddenly supporting her. She had lost. Wearily she turned her face into the rough jacket of the man who held her.

"Oh, Justin, why didn't you listen?"

"Because if I had answered you," Simon said in a low voice, "Major Grahaeme would not now be watching us so confidently. No, don't look up, he's coming after us, which is exactly what I want."

Katherine tried to gather her reeling senses. Why had Simon come instead of Justin? But before she could gather enough breath to ask her questions, Simon deposited her on the ground, saying firmly:

"Stay still and keep quiet." And then he turned to face the man coming up behind them, at the same time taking off the woollen fisherman's hat which had covered his fair hair. Francis stopped, momentarily taken aback, then the pistol in his hand came up to menace Simon.

"No matter . . . you first, then your brother. Where is he, Douglas? Watching us from the safety of that ship out there?"

"No, Major, I am standing directly behind you. Turn round. I want to see your face before I kill you." Justin's voice was like tempered steel as he rose from beneath the sacks at the bottom of the boat where he had been hiding. A moment later the flaming red hair of Jonas Rigg emerged.

Both held pistols aimed directly at Francis, who stared at them in open-mouthed amazement.

"You couldn't have known . . . I gave them no chance to warn you . . ."

"Look behind you at the inn, Major. That piece of red cloth hanging from the window warned me of danger. It has always been a signal known only to my family."

"Barbara," Katherine breathed. Tears of relief were streaming down her cheeks. "But she was hurt – Francis knocked her unconscious . . ."

"Hurt!" Justin's expression was ugly. "If you have harmed her, I swear I will kill you with my bare hands. Simon, go back to the inn, quickly."

"Bring her down here at once," Katherine cried, struggling awkwardly to her knees. "Francis has sent for help, troopers will be here at any moment."

"Kate, your arm!" Justin had just caught sight of the blood on Katherine's sleeve. While Jonas Rigg kept his weapon directed at Francis Grahaeme, he crossed to her side and freed her hands, gathered her into his arms and tore away the thin material.

"It is only a graze," she whispered. "I fell against the rocks. Justin, he meant to kill you and then take me to London, to stand trial with Simon and Barbara. I think his hatred for us has turned his mind. He has killed Mistress Rigg . . . he said it was an accident."

"My God!" The exclamation came from Jonas Rigg. "Meg . . . by your hand . . ." He started towards Francis like a charging bull, his face contorted with grief and fury.

Francis still held his pistol, although he had made no attempt to use it when he had been outnumbered three to one, but the sight of the man bearing down on him like a maddened animal instilled in him fear such as he had never known before, but before he could raise his weapon Jonas Rigg had caught and twisted his arm and he released his hold on it with a howl of pain.

Katherine turned her face against Justin's shoulder as both men rolled over and over in the sand and she saw the innkeeper's hands reaching for Francis's throat. Justin's arms tightened round her trembling shoulders, pressing her against his chest so that she would not be a witness to the last moments of the man who had been determined to destroy their lives. When he at last drew her to her feet, and she forced herself to open her eyes, Jonas was standing over Francis's inert body and she knew, this time, he was dead.

"He deserved to die . . . he killed my Meg," the man said slowly, turning to look at them. The wild light had died out of his eyes; he looked stunned – lost.

"Come with us, Jonas, before the troopers arrive," Justin urged.

"I have something to attend to first. Look, Simon is coming. All of you go back to the ship. If there is time I will join you . . . there is nothing to keep me here now."

Simon was hurrying from the tunnel, Barbara in his arms. She was pale, but smiling. Within minutes they were all in the boat, heading back towards the *Nemesis*. As Justin and his brother rowed, Katherine's eyes followed the tall figure of Jonas Rigg making his way back towards the cliffs and her heart ached.

"What will he do now?" Katherine asked Justin. They stood on the deck of the *Nemesis* as it made for the open sea. A few feet away Jonas stared back at his wife's final resting place in the tiny garden behind the inn. He had not spoken a word to anyone since he had come on board, less than five minutes before the beach was covered with pursuing soldiers.

"Meg was the only stable influence he ever had in his life," Justin returned gently. "He will probably go back to his old ways."

"I wish there was something we could say to him to ease the pain."

"Only time can do that, Kate. Come below, it's chilly for you up here."

Katherine took a last lingering look at the cliffs just visible in the sunlight. She knew it was possible she might never see England again, but she had no regrets. With a smile she put her hand in Justin's. . . .

FRANCESCA

Valentina Luellen

To save her brother from certain death, Francesca is forced into marriage with Raoul de Sebastini, a handsome young mercenary. Too late she discovers he is a half-brother of the notorious Cesare Borgia.

Renowned throughout medieval Europe, the ruthless Borgias are universally feared. Surrounded by their treachery, will Francesca's marriage save her from becoming another of their hapless victims to die by poisoning? One by one, her relatives mysteriously disappear until she is forced to turn for help to the man she trusts least but who attracts her irresistibly – her husband.

— 50p net —

THE FORTUNE-HUNTER

Julia Herbert

Could the elegant young lawyer who came so fortuitously into Amy's life really be no more than a fortune-hunter? He alone can defend her father against the murder charge trumped up by the evil men behind the smuggling ring centred on nearby Poole Harbour. With her father locked up in Winchester Gaol and her mother distraught, Amy comes to rely more and more on Jeffrey Maldon's advice. When the smugglers catch up with him too, Amy finds herself involved in a terrifying race to outwit the "Pegmen" in a desperate bid to save the fortune-hunter's life.

— 50p net —

ALSO AVAILABLE IN MASQUERADE

A ROSE FOR DANGER *by Marguerite Bell*
A smoothly-spoken highwayman is terrorizing the lonely roads around Canterbury when Juliet Ware and her aunt visit friends there for the summer. Torn between her host, the darkly fascinating Sir Nicholas Childe, and the mysterious, but equally attractive Stephen Thorne, Juliet finds herself deeply involved with the intrigue and in danger of becoming one of the highwayman's victims.

THE RUNAWAYS *by Julia Herbert*
In England of 1760, Georgina is abducted by the evil Duke of Quinton. As his magnificent coach sweeps across the West Country to his Wiltshire estates, his pretty prisoner is glimpsed by young Richard Barr. He daringly succeeds in rescuing her from the Duke's clutches, but Georgina's abductor soon picks up the trail of the runaways and a hair-raising chase ensues.

THE SECRET OF VAL VERDE *by Judith Polley*
Antoinette Dubec arrives from France to the war-torn Mexico of 1866 in time to learn of her soldier father's death. The Mexican, Major Chavez, who breaks the news, behaves strangely towards her, but Antoinette is determined to discover how her father died and avenge him. Her investigations lead her into danger, passion and high adventure.

ELEANOR AND THE MARQUIS *by Jane Wilby*
Two cousins, Eleanor and Beatrix, leave their Yorkshire homes to enter fashionable society in London at the time of the Regency. Eleanor is the daughter of a country parson with no prospects, while Beatrix comes from a wealthy family background. Their chaperone in London is an ageing Dowager Duchess who enlists her aristocratic nephew's help in making the poor country girl the toast of the town.

50p net each

To obtain any MASQUERADE title please send your order to:

Mills & Boon Reader Service, P.O. Box 236, 14 Sanderstead Road, South Croydon, Surrey CR2 0YG enclosing your remittance plus 8p per title to cover postage and packing.